REALTOR MIKE BIKE

REALTOR MIKE BIKE

A NONSENSE NOVEL

J O E R E M E S Z

iUniverse, Inc.
Bloomington

REALTOR MIKE BIKE
A Nonsense Novel

iUniverse books may be ordered through booksellers or by contacting:

iUniverse
1663 Liberty Drive
Bloomington, IN 47403
www.iuniverse.com
1-800-Authors (1-800-288-4677)

ISBN: 978-1-4759-0601-1 (sc)
ISBN: 978-1-4759-0602-8 (ebk)

Printed in the United States of America

iUniverse rev. date: 04/04/2012

TO

My Four Sons: John, Vernon, Edward and Steven

With all my love

ABOUT THE AUTHOR

Joe Remesz was born in Bonnyville, Alberta and a professional radio broadcaster for thirty-five years, and a realtor for ten. He began his broadcasting career with the CBC in Toronto after graduating from Lorne Greene's Academy of Radio and Television Arts in 1952.

Remesz has worked throughout Canada and United States spending ten years as news director with radio station CJAT in Trail, British Columbia. He began his real estate career in Penticton, B. C. and now fully retired resides in Edmonton, Alberta and Southern Leyte, Philippines.

Remesz has traveled extensively throughout the world and nuts about the Edmonton Oilers/Eskimos and Toronto Blue Jays.

FOREWARD

REALTOR MIKE BIKE is a work of fiction and, therefore, its characters and the situations in which they find themselves in are entirely my creations. Its setting, on the other hand, is in and around Edmonton, Alberta and places mentioned in the novel are those which I frequented and enjoyed.

I hope you will find REALTOR MIKE BIKE enjoyable and while reading it smile, chuckle and even have a good old-fashioned belly laugh. The novel developed from experiences I encountered as a real estate salesman, my involvement in politics or from incidents I heard about.

I have tried to give credit when ever possible but anecdotes are bandied about so generally and new stories sweep the country so swiftly that it is impossible to discover who put the story in public print first, let alone find out who actually originated it.

CHAPTER 1

Some real estate salesmen are born and some are made and some begin selling real estate but become lost in the competitive world.

Michael (Mike) Bike was a successful commercial salesman but lacked experience in dealing with rural farms and ranches. The 23 year old was employed by the Very Best Realty agency which operated from a suite of offices that were a bit cramped but comfortable on the second floor of an old bank building on Jasper Avenue in Edmonton. The office is a short walk to the City Centre Mall, Sir Winston Churchill Square and the Land Titles office. The rent is cheap, plenty of parking space. Computers and monitors are everywhere. Wires to faxes, copiers and scanners run over the floor in apparent no design. The wall in the lobby entrance is covered with Very Best Realty salesmen including Michael (Mike) Bike.

The central and defining facts of Mike's life were that he was the son of peasants Jan and Paulina Bike who fled Poland in 1928 and as immigrants purchased a $10, 160 acre homestead near Edmonton in order to improve their lifestyle and populate Western Canada. Mike was born three years later on November 8, 1931 the same year that Louise McKinny was the first woman sworn to the Legislative Assembly of Alberta and the first woman elected to the legislature in Canada and the British Empire. It was the same time the average cost of a new home in Edmonton was $4000 and a loaf of bread 20 cents.

Mike's parents wished Ms McKinny the best of luck with her political career and that their only son during the Hungry 30's Depression become a wise man and receives a decent education which they themselves never had.

Mike, this six foot Canadian with black wavy hair, blue eyes, a constant smile and a sensual look may not admit this but earlier in life his parents as immigrants were in a state of poverty and his ambition was to be a hockey player with the Toronto Maple Leafs. But one day while playing the game in High School Mike had a head concussion and because of the injury as an alternate career decided to be a real estate salesman, a career that offers a chance to be creative and while at the right time and the right place, set his goal to be as wealthy as Donald Trump.

As the sun rose over the tranquil city of Edmonton during March 1954 Mike received a phone call to list the Josh Winter farm in nearby Strathcona County. Since Mike had little experience in listing rural properties at the time and wanted experience and perhaps an easier time to find a date than before, thus agreed to list the Winter farm for sale.

Despite his questionable motives as soon as Mike arrived at the farm he noticed that the Mr. and Mrs. Winter were blessed with a large family which included a daughter named Belle who was no more than twenty and had blunt-fingered hands, bright auburn hair, pink cheeks, and blue eyes and wore earrings that looked like rain drops. She also wore sturdy brown sandals and a red-and-white-striped dress.

Belle assisted Mike in holding the tape at one end as he measured the house and barn. While inside the barn Mike found three bottles of milk, got excited and to Belle shouted, "Hey, Bell, look, I found a cow's nest!"

Belle burst into a roar of laughter and while shaking her head said, "Mike, that isn't a cow's nest but three bottles of milk. For a realtor you seem to know little about farming."

Embarrassed, Mike apologized and said, "You are correct with that assessment but I'm willing to learn."

Mike enjoyed dealing in rural properties so much that he had already purchased an acreage at the edge of the city with barn and a two-bedroom cabin on it and where the neighbourhood blue birds and other birds too, each day wished Mike happiness and to be as wealthy as Edmonton billionaire, Daryl Katz.

The cabin was made out of pine logs and had a bedroom which, when it rained, the ceiling went drip, drip, drip.

All the furniture was wrapped in burlap and everything that wasn't was painted black. Mike soon changed that by donating the furniture to the *Salvation Army* and painting the interior three shades of eggshell white. As for the acreage it was near the North Saskatchewan River where one could go boating and fishing.

When the month of May arrived Mike as a hobby decided to make home-brewed beer and from the Winter farm purchased a Jersey cow with a star on her forehead and a huge white curl at the end of her tail. One of her horns curved downwards between her right eye and her ear, and the other small, sharp and thin, curved forward. The cow had big brown eyes which were crossed and not the least a bit gentle. They had a gleam in them, and when Molly was excited became quite wild. Mike also purchased two leghorn chickens.

"Aside from selling real estate I'll do some ranching and brew homemade beer as a hobby," Mike said to his parents and dug a hole in the back yard and buried the chickens like one buries potatoes. Next morning Mike discovered that the chickens were dead.

The following day Mike bought two more chickens but this time planted them upside down. In the morning Mike discovered that the fowl had died also so he wrote a letter to the District Agriculturalist enquiring how to operate a chicken ranch. Within a week Mike received a reply. In part the letter read: "Please send us a soil sample."

As soon as Mike sent the sample he visited the Winter residence every night. Now that he seemed to posses Belle the feelings he had repressed far longer than realized had been freed. Mike could think nothing else but Belle, Belle and Belle. At last it seemed that Mike had Belle for himself and eventually take her out for a date without her parents following her and she told Mike all there is to know about raising chickens including tragic things they face in order not to become a Kentucky Fried Chicken.

Belle said it's the rooster that makes the cock-a-doodle-doo sound, especially in the early morning but it's the hen that lays the eggs out of which come other chicks who eat quantities of grain, often get diseased, picked up by a hawk or even cross the road and get run over by the wheels of a motor vehicle. The rooster is also listed as a month of fortune on the Chinese calendar."

Belle then said, "Chickens also grow faster and lay more eggs while being played music. And it doesn't stop there. With music playing in the background the chickens are less capricious; less agitated and do less feather pecking."

"Cool," Mike said and then asked, "If I were to take a survey among the chickens which type of music do you suggest they would prefer?"

"From experience I find the chickens would show a *cluck* for Country and Western and a *squawk* for rock n roll, Mozart or jazz."

Belle also showed Mike how to do the Chicken Dance and then said, "Mike, here are some pumpkin seeds that you may want to plant in your garden and by the way, can you tell me something about the game of hockey."

Mike said, "OK." But explaining the game to Belle was more trouble than it was worth as everyone in Edmonton seemed to be a hockey authority but still Mike gave several pointers saying that the game is slightly less than a religion and one can listen to Foster Hewitt on the radio describing the game from Maple Leaf Gardens in Toronto which is a perfect setting for fans to enjoy the game and even while watching fall in love.

Before Mike returned to his cabin he had a package of pumpkin seeds, ten hens and a leghorn rooster named Mario. As Mike was setting up the stereo system that played Country and Western music he decided to enjoy some of his newly home brewed beer, poured several bottles into a jug and placed it on the grass beside him.

Since it was a hot and humid day the chickens, led by rooster Mario, felt they were thirsty too and while Mike had his back to them, one by one they put their beaks into the jug swallowing the beer thinking it was herbal water. Minutes later the chickens became emotionally intoxicated and there was a "cock-a-doodle-doo" here and a "cluck, cluck" there. And then a "cock-a-doodle-doo, cluck, cluck everywhere. The chickens then flew onto a fence and Mario onto the rooftop and each fowl cock-a-doodle-doodled and clucked some more.

Ten minutes later they flew back to the lawn where Mike joined them and they did the Chicken Dance, threw kernels of wheat at each other and cock-a-doodle-dood and clucked together until the chickens became sober.

From that day onward the outlook for chicken ranching looked promising and so was brewing home beer as a hobby.

Mike could enjoy pumpkin pie alamode and a milkshake for lunch, bacon and eggs for breakfast, paint the eggs in multi-colours during Easter and eventually enter rooster Mario in the Annual *Crowing Contest* during the Edmonton Rodeo and Farmer's Fall Fair. If Mike was successful in growing a large pumpkin the gourd would be entered at the Big Pumpkin Festival and Weigh-off in Smoky Lake, 72 miles northeast of Edmonton.

Each evening after a busy day at the office it was time for Mike to feed the chickens and milk the cow that was tied to a stake in the middle of the acreage but the rope was so long that Molly soon began scaring the chickens and invading the lawn.

This had a strange effect on the animal. As Mike tried to shorten the rope the cow jabbed him with her horn. When the rope was finally shortened Molly wouldn't stand still and appeared angry and cross-eyed.

Every time Mike came near her hind legs Molly swished her tail and kicked. But she had to be milked. If she wasn't Molly might get milk fever and even die.

One evening after Molly sent the milk pail flying. Belle was summoned and gave Mike instructions on how to properly milk a cow.

Soon milking became relatively easy as the cow kept chewing her cud but one day Mike made a pot of coffee and the cream ruined the flavour.

Although Mike initially knew little about growing pumpkins, chicken ranching or how to milk a cow he knew even less about electricity. This occurred when there was a power failure in rural Edmonton and after spending an hour in darkness instead of phoning the electrical company Mike called on a neighbouring farmer Jerry Fix, who was a handy man, to rectify the problem.

Fix showed up with a hammer and tapped the cabin in several places, when the power suddenly came on.

"Great," Mike said. "How much do I owe you?"

Mike was surprised when Mr. Fix replied, "One-hundred and one dollars."

"One-hundred and one dollars? That's outrages! You spent only a minute tapping the cabin with a hammer. Not only are you a repairman but also a robber. How can you justify such an exorbitant fee?"

"Simple," Mr. Fix said. "My fee for labour is one-dollar and the other one-hundred is for my knowledge where to tap the hammer."

Mike paid the fee but his farming problems compounded because as soon as Fix rectified the electrical problem the cow he purchased started to give sour milk.

Mike called a Vet to see what the trouble was. The Vet informed Mike that the reason the cow was giving sour milk was because the cow eyes were crossed and asked Mike to get a three foot garden hose and that he would arrive at Mike's place within an hour. When the Vet did arrive he put the hose into the cow from behind and started to blow.

After five minutes the cow's eyes were straight. The Vet told Mike that the cow was cured and walked away with a $100 fee.

The milk was pure but a month later the cow became cross-eyed again and produced sour milk. This time Mike didn't want to lose another $100 so he decided to do the doctoring himself.

After blowing for an hour the cow's eyes were still crossed. Mike knew he was doing something wrong and said to himself, "Upon my word, upon my soul I better get in touch with Belle," so he picked up a phone and called Belle for help and told her to blow while he watched the eyes.

As soon as Belle arrived she removed the hose from the rear and turned it around at which point Mike said, "Hey, Belle, what are you doing?"

Belle's reply was, "Mike, you don't expect me to put the same end of the hose in my mouth that you had yours. Do you?"

In the end Molly was cured and again produced excellent milk and cream.

CHAPTER 2

In response that RE/MAX, Century 21 and Royal Le Page were doing more business than the Very Best Realty and Mike was about to reach a pivotal point in his career, his mother suggested the charismatic son might make more sales if he were married. Being a religious type his mother reinforced her suggestion by quoting the Bible: *Be fruitful and multiply, and replenish the earth.*

Reassuring that he could support a wife Mike took his mothers advice seriously to take a chance, be adventurous and find one true love.

Mike wanted to get married but at the same time would settle for anything less than perfection and the wife be the centrepiece of his life.

A search ended however, when Mike was determined to make the most of this moment and asked Belle to help him with the sick cow, which gave sour milk for the third time and said to her, "Belle, you are adorable."

"And so are you. I think you are sweet," Belle said, "I feel that I have known you for a long time. The only fault I can detect in you is your tendency to smile too much."

As soon as the cow problem was rectified Mike fell madly in love with Belle and there, on the farm, inside the barn with Molly mooing, hens clucking and Mario crowing, proposed marriage. A bond was sealed as soon as Belle said, "Mike, oh, dear. I thought you would never ask. You are patient and loving. I don't think I couldn't ask for more. Certainly, I would be delighted to be Mrs. Bike for the rest of my life and even afterward."

That's when instead of a fancy, expensive engagement ring; Mike presented his wife-to-be a giant foam hand that read, "Belle. You Are #1."

With time Mike found Belle responsible and her imagination fertile. She, like Mike, enjoyed farming; drinking beer and she could hum every Hank Williams tune. On occasion Belle sang Country and Western songs at the *Cook County Saloon* and gave singing lessons at Night School.

On the minus side Belle always wanted a German shepherd dog like the one she had but ran away. Belle was temperamental and at times seemed insecure. That insecurity eventually disappeared when Belle invited Mike to her parents' farm for a barbecue. The barbecue was a great success because that evening in a flutter of passion Mike's and Belle's love recipe of two hearts full of admiration, promising to love and cry together until death, merged. Minutes later Mike and Belle announced their wedding date for November 15, 1955 a time when the world population was nearly 3-billion and Canadian stand-up comedian Howie Mandel was one-day old.

The following week Mike and Belle sent out wedding invitations but when J. M. Swintak. Manager at the Fairmont McDonald Hotel got his had difficulty figuring out the meaning of the abbreviation RSPV. Swintak pondered and pondered and finally asked his wife who said, "RSPV? I know what that means."

"Oh ya, what?"

"It means to remember send vedding presents."

A day after Swintak found out what RSPV meant Mike met farmer Jerry Fix on the street and invited him to the wedding.

"Sure, I'll come," Fix said.

"Great. Do you know how to get to the No Name Universal Church?"

"I do."

"Well, when you get there, make sure you ring the front door with your elbow."

"Elbow?"

"You are going to bring presents, aren't you?"

Fix said that he would.

One week before the wedding the kitchen staff at the *Mac* Hotel went on strike for higher wages so Belle and Mike had to rent a hall and arrange a meal, which included North Saskatchewan River fish that had to be picked up and delivered to the Norwood Community hall.

"The stress of going through a wedding is unbelievable. I didn't think that things could go wrong," Belle said to Mike but they did as the wedding day approached. No event in the in the City of Champions was more exciting than Mike's and Belle's wedding, not the Eskimos winning the Grey Cup, the Oilers the Stanley Cup or even the Queen's or the Pope Paul 11 visit.

For their honeymoon bride and groom traveled to Jasper National Park to do some leisurely skiing. Unfortunately Belle was involved in a skiing accident when she went out of control, missed a tree but struck an adjacent chalet. When the ambulance arrived it took Belle to the hospital where a waiting doctor in Emergency said, "We'll have to take Mrs. Bike for an x-ray."

Mike who followed the ambulance in his yellow Chevy said, "Do that while I wait in the hallway."

One-hour later the doctor approached Mike and appeared embarrassed. Mike immediately thought the doctor had made a mistake and Belle had died while under an anaesthetic.

"Dead? Heck, no," the doctor said, "Your bride has regained consciousness and is in a wonderful frame of mind. Do you want to see her?"

"Please."

As Ed entered the recovery room Belle's first words weren't *Merry Christmas* or *How do I look*? But, "Mike, why don't you go and list the chalet which immobilized me?"

"Which chalet?"

"The one up the mountain which distracted me as I was reading a banner on the balcony which reads, *Humbug with Christmas*."

"I'll do that," Mike said and drove back to the mountain to try and list the chalet but a realtor who gets a tip from someone else must act quickly.

By the time Mike reached the chalet the old sign was changed to a new one, which advised everyone: *Under New Management.*

It took Belle until Valentine's Day in February to fully recover from her skiing accident. "The flowers and chocolates Mike showered on me were a good source of therapy," Belle said to anyone who enquired about the state of her health.

Belle was so healthy that when March 17th arrived not only her lips but also her eyes were smiling at a St. Patrick's party in the *Petroleum Club* which was decorated with shamrocks.

Dressed in their best with as many touches of green as possible the MC had Mike and Belle and others too, singing: *When Irish Eyes Are Smiling, Where the River Shannon's flowing* and *My Wild Irish Rose.*

After a participant recited *Finnigan to Flannigan* the MC told a story how St. Patrick got rid of the snakes in Ireland.

Before the social evening came to an end a smorgasbord of nutritional good sense was held and featured all one could drink of Mike's home-brewed beer which he had coloured green for the occasion.

At any rate the party epitomized at least two aspects of Mike's character that was taking him to the top of his profession—devotion to his wife and the power of instant decision.

Three days later spring officially arrived and pussy willows had their kittens and migratory birds were heading north to nest. It was a time wild roses in and around Edmonton began to bloom and pollinate.

"It's definitely spring time," Belle said to Mike while they were cleaning the front yard.

"Because it's time to go camping?" Mike asked.

"No."

"Then how did you reach that conclusion?"

"Because I'm the only one in our household who scoops up doggie poo left on our front lawn."

As Easter weekend approached Mike and Belle celebrated the holiday as if it was another Christmas and they had a lot of things to do: unpack, the Christmas tree and decorate it with Easter lights, which were multi-coloured and shaped like Easter eggs. Pussy willows and oh-so-adorable bunnies were used to decorate the tree. Mind you many of the bunnies were made of plastic imported from China where labour making such things was cheap, much cheaper compared to Canada and America.

While decorating the tree Mike and Belle sat by candle light and listened to the radio and the latest releases a disc jockey hadn't played before including: *Rockin n Rollin with an Easter Bunny, Mommy Forgot To Put Yeast in the Hot Cross Buns* and *The Vegreville Easter Egg is Big but Not Bigger than Biggar, Saskatchewan*.

After several days of running around, Belle exclaimed, "Whew! I'm exhausted. Easter is a hectic time of the year!"

"It certainly is a spring-like fling with retailers looking for customers to make their cash registers ring," Mike said and went on, "A difference I notice, however, is that instead of saying 'Merry Christmas' the clerks say 'Happy Easter' and inside the Kingsway Mall an Easter Bunny instead of Santa Clause sits in a chair and says to children sitting on his knees, 'What will you have for Easter this year?'"

When Easter day arrived the first thing Mike and Belle did was to attend a sunrise church service and listen to Pastor Taylor at the No Name Universal Church tell an ancient story about a *Superior* who died on a cross for all those living on Planet Earth. Although one could not see the sun rising in the horizon because of fog, *ecumenism* was still a popular word and that it was a universal feast of a child born on Christmas day, grew into adulthood, died on a Friday and rise from the dead on a Sunday.

As soon as the Easter sunrise service was over the bride and groom drove to their cabin and exchanged Easter gifts. Belle received a white-coloured sweater from Mike along with a bouquet of lilies and an Easter card, which read: "Belle. You Are My Easter Lilly Friskier Than A Two-Year-Old Filly."

Ed in turn received a pair of rubber boots from Belle along with a bouquet of daffodils. A short time later Mike and Belle drove to Mike's parent's home where they enjoyed a buffet style lunch featuring delicious ham, scalloped potatoes, hot cross buns all one could eat of insect-like things: lobster, crab, clam, oyster, mussel and shrimp.

Mike and Belle did not stay long because his parents were preparing their car for the Easter Parade of antique cars. They were already dressed in period costumes to go with their 1912 Cadillac. After exchanging gifts with his parents Ed and Belle drove home to take part in the *Great Easter Egg Hunt* sponsored by the *Chamber of Commerce* which participants on a stretch of country road, like Sherlock Holmes, had to use their brain and eyes to solve all the clues and claim the big prize—a three-foot tall chocolate rabbit. There was a sack full of multi-coloured chicken eggs for the runner-up.

Although chickens in Edmonton were working overtime laying eggs Mike and Belle didn't win a prize because they misread a clue and ended at the Cooking Lake Hunting and Golfing Resort where Mike tried on his rubber boots.

According to Belle the boots were the best invention yet conceived. These were Grade-A gumboots like Belle's grandpa wore many years ago when Planet Earth was still green and he used horses to pull out a tractor when it got stuck in a soggy field near a slough.

As soon as April showers turned to May and flowers and the grass had riz Belle often wondered where Mike is. Well, Mike was a promoter and when he wasn't in Edmonton, he would be in Toronto and even New York trying to raise money and floating loans.

But because of his real estate inexperience Mike's career continued at a slow place.

There's no human impulse greater for a realtor than the urge to own his/her own real estate. Mike wanted to purchase revenue-producing properties for him and Belle but his first crises occurred because lack of funding.

Mike's first desire was to purchase, after obtaining a loan from a bank, a 26-unit apartment complex that he hoped to renovate, jack up the rent and then sell at a profit.

To apply for a mortgage loan Mike had to see the manager of a bank, in this case it was the Alberta Treasury Bank, where he introduced himself to the receptionist and said, "Can I please speak to the manager, alone?"

"Yes," she said, "I'll fetch him."

The manager introduced himself as John Brown, a calm man in his forties.

"You are the manager?" Mike asked.

"I am."

"Then can I speak to you in private."

"Certainly," and led Mike to the manager's office, closed the door behind him and turned the key in the lock.

"Now that we are alone, how can I help you?" Brown asked.

"I need to open an account and request a mortgage loan."

"For what amount?"

"Fifteen thousand dollars."

Mike fidgeted in his chair while Mr. Brown reviewed a mortgage application and then said, "Mike, your assets seem to be in order. How about your liabilities?"

Mike said that he could lie with the best of them and his ambition was to become a wealthy entrepreneur like Harry Bronfman was during the 1930's Depression.

The banker took that to mean that aside from selling real estate Mike was also bootlegging his home-brewed beer so the loan was approved without difficulty.

Sunset Place was a 40-year-old three-story wood-frame structure in north Edmonton where at one time it was the favourite place to live but over the year's crime, drugs and urban blight eroded the district. *Sunset Place* had a leaking tar roof, stucco siding and a gravel parking lot. It was a walk-up with a reputation for alcohol abuse, poverty and violence, where elderly female tenants amused themselves by knitting guns and 12-year-old boys were trafficking in drugs. The building stood in a crime-ridden neighbourhood near a park where homeless people hung out. A used car lot, a pawnshop and the dilapidated York Hotel, which had a rough reputation because of its clientele, are situated nearby.

Edmonton police recently published a weekend of criminal activities in the Edmonton Boyle Street community where they were called upon to investigate:

> 12 stolen vehicles, 11 fights in bars, 10 false security alarms, 9 B and E's, 8 purse snatchings, 7 marital disturbances, 6 obscene phone calls, 5 fraudulent, money grabbing, solicitations, 4 stabbings, 3 child abductions, 2 homicides and a rescue of a cat which had climbed a tree and refused to come down.

Shortly after the mortgage was approved Mike asked Belle if she would like to manage *Sunset Place* but after seeing the condition the building was in, she declined.

"Then what would you like to do as a career?"

"Well, I don't want to be a landlord or sell real estate. Eventually I want to become a newspaper columnist or a manager at Tourist resort."

"And as a columnist what would you write about?"

"Global warming and the deteriorating state of the Planet Earth."

"I'm certain that by becoming an apartment manger you'll pick up enough material for at least 100 columns," Mike said.

Belle still refused to become a landlord, which if one were to make a list of most unpopular professions, would have to rank with that of a telephone solicitor, an investigative news reporter and a door-to-door salesman.

Mike was persuasive and following a spirited conversation reminded Belle about the marriage vow she had taken so she finally compromised to become a landlord but on three conditions. (1) That Mike change the name of the apartment building from *Sunset Place* to *Edbelle Manor* (2) that Belle become a non-resident manager and (3) that from now onward her name be hyphened to read Belle Winter-Bike which became a joke in the neighbourhood because of the cold weather in Edmonton only a handful rode a bicycle during winter.

Belle's experience as a landlord began when a tenant moved into a one-bedroom Edbelle apartment and hosted a warm-up party whose theme was, "As many people in a small unit as possible." This was a major success and confirmed by the number of policemen ultimately involved following a phone call to 911 and fistfights and broken glass and furniture, which preceded the call.

Belle was out to be a Kind Lady type of a landlord and listened to tenants' complaints acknowledging them immediately. As it turned out, besides being a landlord

Belle soon became a plumber, which was unfortunate because the building was equipped with antiquated fixtures. Also inappropriate items kept mysteriously lodged in the toilet.

Belle would respond to a toilet alarm in the middle of the night using a mechanical snake, retrieving items that plugged the toilet. Items like: female sanitary pads, fish heads, bowling shoes and stripped marijuana plants.

When Belle would show the items to the tenants they always appeared to be amazed and blamed the lodged articles on previous tenants.

Soon Belle found out that it wasn't easy being a Kind Lady landlord and it didn't help that one-half of the tenants in Edbelle Manor were on social assistance and viewed paying rent as an optional part of a Rental Agreement. When the rent was over due, and Belle came to collect it, the tenant would say something like, "I had the money yesterday but you weren't around." It was said in an accusing tone of voice suggesting that it was Belle's fault for not showing up at a time they had the money thereby leaving no option but buy cases of beer or going to bingo games.

One tenant instead of paying his rent bought several cases of beer and fell asleep on a couch leaving a frying pan full of hamburger meat on a stove element set at *High*. Soon smoke filled the second-story apartment, triggering a smoke detector and then the fire alarm covering the entire building. As soon as the firemen arrived this tenant was led to an ambulance and treated for smoke inhalation.

When the tenant was released he said to another tenant, "The fire alarm began ringing at 1:30 a. m. but we had a false alarm last week so I kept sleeping until someone hollered, *Fire* and there was a knock on my door. It was then that I noticed tenants waiting outside cuddling their cats and puppies under their coats."

At 3:00 a. m. Belle received a phone call from the Fire Chief who said Edbelle Manor had been on fire.

"Fortunately the blaze was confined to the tenant's unit and was put out within several minutes."

The following day when Belle asked the tenant the circumstances of the fire he said, "I saw a ghost on the balcony, maybe he's the one who did it."

Belle pointed to the empty beer bottles. "How did the empty bottles get there?"

"I don't know," the tenant said. "I never bought an empty bottle of beer in my entire life."

The unit which had the fire needed an immediate paint job so Belle asked a painter for an estimate. "What will you charge to paint this unit?"

After giving an estimate of $200 Belle exclaimed, "I wouldn't pay Michelangelo that much!"

"Listen missus," the painter said, "If Michael Angelo is doing the job for less, and he's not a member of a union."

Belle believed in unions and let the painter paint the apartment.

As a landlord Belle often received complaints from tenants. Since she became a landlord they were:

1. The bathroom faucet doesn't work and would you mind having the hole in the roof shifted over the tub.
2. I don't want to complain but yesterday I made a batch of cookies and they were eaten in five minutes, by mice.
3. I'm moving today and my lease agreement says to leave the suite in exactly the same condition in which I found it when I moved in. That's why I filled the unit with 1000 cockroaches.

4. I told you the unit was filled with roaches. Why did you raise the rents claiming they were pets?
5. My suite has cross ventilation—a hole in the ceiling and another in the floor.
6. When I phoned saying there was a mouse in my apartment you replied 'Send him down to sign a Rental Agreement' How come?
7. There's an airlock in the building plumbing system. I can't sleep at nights because of the ratta—tatta-tatta sound throughout the building.
8. A stranger keeps knocking on my door at 2:00 a. m. asking for a cigarette.
9. My screen door is ripped and cracks round the door and windows let in a draft and all sorts of insects.
10. The washing machine in the Laundry Room is on the blink again.
11. The toilet is blocked and we cannot bathe the children until is is cleared.
12. I want to complain about the farmer across the street. Every morning at 5:30 his cock wakes me up. And it's getting too much.
13. The toilet seat is cracked: where do I stand?
14. I'm writing on behalf of my sink, which is running away from the wall.
15. I request your permission to remove my drawers in the kitchen.
16. Our lavatory seat is broken in half and is now in three pieces.
17. Will you please send someone to mend our cracked sidewalk? Yesterday my wife tripped on it and is now pregnant.

18. Will you please send someone to look at my water; it's funny colour and not fit to drink.
19. Our kitchen sink is very damp, we have two children and would like a third, so will you please send someone to do something about it?
20. Could you please send someone to fix our bath faucet? My wife got her toe stuck in it and it is very uncomfortable for us.
21. This is to let you know that there is a strange smell coming from next door
22. The tenant next door has a large erection in his back garden, which is unsightly and dangerous.

On about the 15th of each month Belle would usually be hit for a loan by some of the tenants. Most often the reasons for one were:

1. Welfare cheque had not arrived or was already used up.
2. Play bingo.
3. Bus fare.
4. Repair a bicycle.
5. Purchase cigarettes.
6. Attend a wrestling match.
7. Pay an outstanding bill with a TV cable company.
8. Attend a funeral.
9. Bail relative out of jail.
10. Purchase tampons.

Belle soon developed a policy about handing out loans to tenants. She would say something like, "I have made arrangements with a bank. The bank doesn't find me tenants and I don't make loans."

If this wouldn't work Belle would quote Shakespeare or was it Ben Franklin, and say, "Neither lender or borrower be."

If that still didn't work Belle would quote D. H. Lawrence and use the four-lettered word beginning with F and adding to it the word "off."

Tenants living in Edbelle Manor didn't know much about each other but one couldn't have cabbage, dried salted fish or curry for dinner without everyone in the complex finding out.

Belle encountered several tense moments as a landlord. The first occurred when a tenant moved out without giving notice or paying rent and then raw sewage filled the basement suit. Belle scraped the guck with a shovel and placed it in the back of a pickup she thought belonged to the tenant.

Unfortunately Belle discovered the following day the pickup did not belong to the tenant but to the Champion City used car lot. The vehicle had been stolen and abandoned.

And there was the time Belle evicted a couple for non-payment of rent. The furniture, linen and piano were placed on the lawn outside near the street. This done the husband placed his head between his hands and became depressed while his wife played the piano merrily making several of the neighbours annoyed.

A short time later a policeman arrived and asked the wife, "How come your husband is depressed and you are so happy?"

The wife looked up at the policeman and replied, "Gordon and I have been married for twenty-five years and his the first time we are out together."

Following this eviction Belle developed a Late Rent *Collection Policy*—to seize, sue or evict. From that moment the first tenant who didn't pay his or her monthly $300 rent on time Belle sued and after following court rules, seized the furniture which was handed to a liquidation auctioneer who sold it a loss 10 cents on a dollar.

For his fee the auctioneer took another 10%, which now left Belle with $27, not counting her cartage expense.

Following this unprofitable experience Belle said to Ed, "Not worth the hassle. I'm not a landlord because it will improve my health. Next time, I'll sue the tenant."

And when Belle did she paid the Court clerk $10 and handed the tenant a writ stating to appear at a Small Claims Court on a certain date.

The tenant did appear in Court but the judge who had a large family of his own said, "Tenant, I know you have a wife and family to take care of. I'm giving you another two weeks to pay your debt."

When the two weeks expired the tenant failed to appear in Court, abandoned the apartment in the middle of the night and disappeared into Never, Never Land.

Now Belle was out of pocket, a $10 processing fee, another two weeks rent of $150 for a total of $460. She had to dish out another $50 to have the carpet, stove, bathroom and the apartment walls, which were spray-painted with ketchup and mustard, cleaned.

When the next tenant was $300 delinquent Belle said, "Aha, I'm going to garnishee his/her wages" and she did, by handing the tenant's employer a notice stating that part of the wages the tenant earned rightfully belonged to Edbelle Manor.

Belle was surprised however, that according to the employer, he wasn't paying any wages to the tenant but to a numbered company, which he refused to divulge. Before Belle could trace who owned the numbered company and who were the shareholders, the employer went bankrupt and skipped town.

The only recourse Belle had while dealing with delinquent tenants was to hand one an eviction notice. "Let's be practical. The other methods of collecting rent aren't working Belle said to Ed. "The best recourse is to give a tenant and eviction notice."

"Go ahead," Ed said, "We might as well make the most of an unpleasant situation."

Belle handed the next delinquent tenant a regular 30-day eviction notice of the second day of delinquency but the tenant challenged the eviction.

Both Belle and the tenant appeared in Court and the same judge, the one with the large family, said to the tenant, "Due to the downturn in the economy I extend your tenancy for another week, that's it."

But before the week extension expired the tenant trashed the apartment leaving it in a terrible mess which included spray paint on each wall with derogatory words.

This time Belle was out of pocket more than $700 and the tenant disappeared.

The following day Belle arrived at the apartment building at 8:00 a. m. and as a routine checked the entrance doors that they opened and closed properly and then the hallways and stairway of each floor for burnt out lights, fire alarms, pizza cartons left in the garbage chutes and no drunk sleeping in one of the corridors. As part of her daily routine, Belle next went to the basement to check on the furnace settings and the hot water tanks.

On this occasion Belle was surprised when she found strangers sleeping on the concrete floor, black plastic bags gathered around them. Seeing the intruders all Belle said was, "Good morning everyone," and hurried to her office where she called the cops who were on the scene within minutes.

As Belle led the cops into the basement furnace room six Street People in the late teens and early twenties, two female, both pregnant, and four male, were found with burglary tools, pepper spray, knives and drug paraphernalia lying by their side and explicit graffiti in black and red scribbled throughout the four walls, even on the ceiling. Seeing the cops a male tried to escape and ran out the basement rear door.

One of the cops gave chase and eventually caught him while jumping over a concrete retaining wall. After identifying themselves the homeless were taken outside where by a paddy wagon they were each handcuffed, questioned and burglary tools, knives and drugs seized as evidence.

But that wasn't the only time Belle wasn't free from grief and anxiety. Three days later at 2:00 a. m. police raided apartment #11 and seized a large quantity of marijuana and hashish.

The seizure was the result after the two female tenants, Nichol and Emily, better known as Wheezy and Sneezy in the neighbourhood, had an argument and Wheezy after abandoning her mate, ratted to the police drug squad. When police arrived at Edbelle Manor they knocked on the door of unit 11 but hearing no response, and if Sneezy was home, there would be time for her to flush the abuse substances down the toilet, kicked in the door. The cops, both male, with a flashlight in hand searched every part of the suite: heating registers, cupboards, light fixtures, etc.

It wasn't until they entered the bedroom and found Sneezy hiding in the closet frightened and the hashish and marijuana wrapped under the bed. Sneezy was charged with possession and trafficking in drugs. She was let go on her own recognizance and next day, left what furniture she had behind and fled.

Although collecting rent from tenants had been stressful at times. Belle possessed a quality which many landlords lack, a sense of humour, even the time she incorrectly installed a new fertilizer flap on the fertilizer spreader but leaving the flap wide open.

Belle had spread 10 pounds of fertilizer on the lawn when she realized her mistake and the cleaning lady came up with a solution and said, "Belle, that much fertilizer will kill the grass. Why don't use the vacuum cleaner and pick up some of the tiny pebbles?"

It worked perfectly but the sight of vacuuming one's lawn was an unusual one in Edmonton so much so that traffic slowed down. One driver ran up the sidewalk hitting a light pole, another missed his turn but kept circling the block, finally stopping in front of Belle and asked, "Is that good for the lawn?"

"Of course," Belle said, "Vacuuming picks up the grass and helps to aerate the lawn at the same time."

"Good. Good. When I get home I'll try to do the same," the driver said. And if he did the driver may have experienced what Belle did. He would have to buy a new vacuum cleaner.

One may say Belle had a sense of humour but so did several of her tenants. This occurred when an amateur musician was making horrendous sounds with his saxophone and Belle knocked on his door. As soon as there was a "Come in," Belle entered the apartment, yanked the instrument out of the tenant's hands and said, "Don't you know there's a little old lady in the suite above you?"

"I don't think so. Would you mind humming the few first bars and then I'll be able to play the tune for you," the tenant said.

Then there was the time a tenant phoned Belle in the middle of the night complaining that the smoke detector in his apartment was so sensitive that it had gone off for the umpteenth time.

"Maybe it's the smoke from your cigarette that's causing the smoke detector to go off so often," Belle suggested. "When did it go off the last time?"

"The last time it went off was when I farted."

As autumn approached Edbelle Manor had an intricate intercom system in that if one wanted access to apartment number 09 he/she would have to buzz 119.

To get access to apartment number 22 one would have to buzz number 132. In other words there was a difference of 110 and often this was confusing to say the least especially if one didn't use the buzzer but grabbed the entrance door while someone else was either entering or leaving the complex.

In that case the visitor would wander up and down the hallways looking for an apartment number, which did not correspond with the number posted on the intercom. This confusion increased when one day following a severe thunder and lightning storm the entire intercom system was out of order. A telephone repairman was called and initially even he couldn't figure out how the intercom operated.

Minutes before the repairman arrived there was a heated verbal exchange between a tenant in number 21, a bank employee by the name Rita Rowe, and a visitor who wanted access to suite number 17, which if the conversation was transcribed should have been stored in the National Archives in Ottawa for future generations to study the subject of annoyance.

Ms Rowe, a single parent, a bank teller at the TD Bank lived in #21 on the third floor. The main entrance door and the intercom system were below. A visitor wanted access to suite number 17 and buzzed what she thought was the correct number 127 but unfortunately the phone rang in the suite occupied by Ms Rowe.

The phone ringing was the umpteenth time with in a space of an hour and Ms Rowe became understandably annoyed and would respond with something like, "What's the matter with you? There is no Shirley Yankton living here. You crazy or something?"

The visitor buzzing the number apologized and said it wasn't her fault the suite number she buzzed rang elsewhere. "I'll try again." And when she did Ms Rowe's number rang a second time.

Expletives were exchanged and the disgruntled visitor finally left without reaching her friend.

When Ms Rowe's phone rang a third time she leaned over the balcony railing and with all her strength dumped a bucket of water on the male's head and shoulders. As it turned out the caller was Rabbi Libowitch who had an appointment with a member of his congregation to discuss an upcoming *Talmud Torah* meeting.

It took the repairman most of the afternoon to figure out what had caused the relays in the intercom to malfunction. Early next day the mystery was solved when a previously evicted tenant admitted that he had sprayed the buzz numbers with Ed's home-brewed beer.

As for Ms Rowe in 21, she got locked out in the balcony because when she poured a bucket of water on Rabbi Libowitch's head, a blast of cold air closed the door behind her.

To make matters worse, her three-year-old son was inside the apartment and upon hearing his mother using bad words, dropped rolls and rolls of toilet paper into the toilet bowl and flushing them. Soon the toilet overflowed and the bathroom turned into a mini-swimming pool.

It was at this point that another tenant phoned Belle at home and by the time she arrived at Edbelle Manor Ms Rowe was still on her balcony, frantic and a 30-foot drop to the pavement below was to risky to jump. There was nothing Ms Rowe could do except watch the passing vehicles and the people going in and out of the apartment building.

Seeing Belle Ms Rowe suggested Belle call 911.

But since Belle had a master key Belle thought she would use it to open the apartment entrance door.

This took another ten minutes however, because Ms. Rowe had placed a security chain inside, which when opened, had only enough space for a hand to go through.

Seeing the difficulty Ms Rowe was in Belle grabbed a chisel and a hammer prying the door casing from the wall and eventually rescued the desperate Ms Rowe.

As soon as Ms Rowe was rescued she picked up a clothes hanger, pulled out globs and globs from the toilet bowl and then mopped the bathroom floor.

There was little mopping necessary, however, because by now the water made its way to the bathroom of the tenant below.

Seeing and hearing water dripping from his bathroom ceiling this particular tenant marched straight up a flight of stairs and knocked on Ms Rowe's door. When Ms Rowe poked her head out the tenant screamed, "Look, Ms Rowe! You know nothing about disciplining children!"

Ms Rowe shot back, "Stop your screaming! It's because of tenants like you that I'm moving out and live in a better neighbourhood!"

"So am I," the tenant growled.

"You mean to say you are moving out too?"

"No." the tenant replied, "With you gone, Edbelle Manor will be a better neighbourhood."

It's not the first time Ms Rowe got into trouble as a tenant at Edbelle Manor. A week earlier she had an accident when she tried to open the door to go to work at the bank and the key broke off in the lock. After resorting in vain to screwdrivers and pliers she decided to call a locksmith who arrived promptly and as she looked through the peephole said to him, "My key broke off inside in the lock."

"On the inside? It will take at least an hour and I'll have to charge you fifty-dollars."

"I don't have $50 in the apartment right now but as soon as I get out, I'll go to the bank and pay you."

"I'm very sorry, mam," the locksmith articulated with instructive courtesy. "I'm afraid that as a charter member of the Edmonton Locksmith's Union and one who helped draw up the last Collective Agreement I'm prohibited from unlocking your door unless I'm paid in advance."

"You're joking of course."

"The subject of the Locksmith's Union is no joking manner. In drawing up the Collective Agreement no detail has been overlooked and clause number 7 says 'Gold shall open doors, and the doors shall adore it."

"Please," Ms Rowe pleaded. "Be reasonable. Open the door for me and since I have no cash on hand I'll use my credit card."

"I'm sorry Ms Rowe. Our company doesn't accept credit cards and further more there are ethics involved. Have a good day."

And with that the locksmith made his exit.

Bewildered Ms Row called the bank where she worked and informed her supervisor that she probably wouldn't be able to come to work that day and called another locksmith, and just in case, said to herself, "I'm not going to say I have no money until after he opens the door for me."

Ms Rowe then searched the *Yellow Pages* directory and dialed a number.

"What address?" a guarded receptionist asked.

". . . Street. Apartment 21."

The receptionist hesitated and asked Ms Rowe to repeat the address and then said, "The place where you are calling from, is it Edbelle Manor?"

"It is."

"Impossible. The Edmonton Locksmiths' Union prohibits us from doing any work at that address."

Before another word was said the receptionist hung up.

So Ms Rowe went to *Yellow Pages* again and made another dozen calls to other locksmiths and the instant they heard the address and the mention of Edbelle Manor, they all refused to do the job.

To find a solution elsewhere Ms Rowe called the Edbelle Manor janitor and he replied, "In the first place, I don't know how to open locks, and in, in the second, even if I did know, I wouldn't do it since my job is cleaning the place and not letting suspicious birds out of their cages."

Ms Rowe then called the bank, in the hope that her supervisor could come and open the door. "Bad luck," the supervisor said, "So you can't get out of your apartment? You just never run out of excuses not to come to work"

At this point Ms Rowe had a homicidal urge. She hung up, called the bank again and asked for a co-worker, Noel Laporte, that she knew well and a bit brighter than her superior.

Sure enough Noel seemed interested in finding a solution. "Tell me, was it the key or the lock that broke?"

"The key. Half of it is inside the lock. The doorknob won't turn left or right."

'Didn't you try to get the piece that's stuck inside out with a set of pliers or a screw driver?"

"I tried both, but it's impossible."

"Then you'll have to call a locksmith."

"I already did but they want payment in advance."

"So pay him and there you are."

"But, don't you see. I have no money with me."

"You sure have problems. Sorry but I can't help you," Noel said and hung up.

And so ended that day but on the second Ms Rowe got up early to begin making more phone calls. But something she found quite frequent, not only the intercom but also the telephone was out of order. Problem: how to request repair service without a telephone to place a call? She went onto the balcony and began shouting at people walking along the street. The street noise was deafening. At most, an occasional person would raise his head distractedly and then continue.

Next she placed sheets of paper and carbons in the typewriter and composed the following message: Madam or Sir: My key has broken off in the lock. This is the second day that I'm locked inside my apartment. If you find this, please help me. I'm at Edbelle Manor unit #21."

Ms Rowe made the sheets of paper into little airplanes and threw them over the railing and they fluttered a long time. Some with the help of a wind flew long distances, some were run over by non-stop vehicles, some landed on awnings of other buildings but one dropped on the sidewalk where a diminutives gentleman picked it up and read it. He then looked up towards the balcony shading his eyes with his left hand.

Ms Rowe put on a friendly face but the gentlemen tore the paper into many little pieces and with an irate gesture hurled them into the gutter. Seconds turned into a minute, minutes turned into hours but Ms Rowe continued throwing paper plane messages from the balcony but they either weren't read, or if they were, weren't taken seriously.

By late afternoon an envelope was slipped under Ms Rowe's apartment door. The telephone company cut off her service for non-payment. Then in succession they cut off her gas, electricity and water and that's when Ms Rowe got irate and with her fist continuously banged on her door causing noise that reverberated in the entire second floor.

Hearing the commotion the tenant next door summoned Belle who eventually called a locksmith, paid in advance, had the amount added to Ms Rowe's Security Deposit. This done the lock was repaired, a new key cut and the door opened.

Belle kept an Edbelle Manor Tenant/Landlord Diary, which highlighted each day of the month with an interesting event or two for the record. Here is a sample of Belle's diary for the month of June.

DATE IN JUNE 1956 HIGHLIGHT

1. Tenant in apartment 02 left for France today with her employer. Back in August.
2. Marigolds at the front entrance of Edbelle Manor finally in bloom.
3. Tenant in 07 complains that she has a large insect crawling on her kitchen counter. I call a termite exterminator but he says the object isn't an insect but a crab waiting to be cooked in boiling water.
4. Tenant in #19 says she saw mice in her suite. I call exterminator again and he says they aren't mice but bats seeking shelter in the attic of Edbelle Manor.
5. I begin a study of bats by attaching a tiny radio transmitter with surgical glue on the back of six bats.
6. A disturbance erupts in #24. Cops charge common-law husband with beating his wife.
7. Tenant in #07 says she's unable to pay her rent because her six-month-old child flushed the welfare cheque down the toilet.

8. A swarm of wasps lands on the kitchen light fixture of #21. I call exterminator again and he says why the wasps swarmed were because the tenant was wearing too much hair spray and underarm deodorant.
9. Tenant in #15 has car stolen. Tenant in #17 has purse snatched near the library.
10. Tenant in #11 has a dream that she was eaten up by a talking toilet.
11. Phone 911 when tenant occupying #13 found lying on the hallway floor near her door. Paramedic says the tenant had developed tridecaphobia.
12. Two year-old child of tenant #16 found sleeping inside the dryer in the laundry room. Luckily he didn't try the microwave oven.
13. Someone used a corner in the hallway as a toilet. Cleaning lady refused to clean the poo even when I offered her a gas mask.
14. Tenant in #12 has rental cheque returned NSF.
15. Read in the paper about the Springhill, Nova Scotia mine disaster.
16. Tenant in # 21 has key broken in her door, all sorts of problems.
17. Edmonton has mosquito attack. I discover in my neck a gland that secretes profanity as I slap and slap.
18. Tenant in #19 writes a Notice of Objection after I give him an eviction notice.
19. Lawnmower keeps dying because the grass is so high. I couldn't cut the grass earlier because it rained for two straight weeks.

20. First day of summer. Listen to the radio as Tommy Douglas of the CCF wins 4th consecutive majority during a provincial election.
21. Tenant in #21 enquires if Edbelle Manor allows snakes. Tenant won a cobra in a bantam hockey team raffle.
22. Attend wedding of tenants in #17. The couple have lived common-law for 23 years.
23. Tenant in #02 has holiday in Europe cut short. Employer has heart attack and unable to continue journey.
24. My study of bats in attic is complete. Research shows bats often commit an en mass suicide.
25. Tenant in #02 says she's pregnant.
26. Marigolds landscaping front entrance of Edbelle Manor disappear overnight. I replace the flowers with plastic petunias.
27. Remove pigeon droppings from entrance door.
28. Cat in # 12 scratches a hole through the litter box and the floor.
29. School out. Live-in kids terrorize Edbelle Manor with graffiti, some with vulgar words.
30. Time to pay property taxes.

CHAPTER 3

In order to keep Edbelle Manor fully occupied Belle ran an ad in the *Journal* during weekends. One weekend Belle advertised a *lush* apartment for rent but a prospect didn't believer her, that is, until he tripped over a drunk in the hallway. This particular tenant was a terror when drunk. When sober he was all right, kind of simple wouldn't hurt a fly, nicest tenant in Edbelle Manor. But when he got drunk—Whoo! To make matters worse when he sobered up he complained that the walls in his apartment were so thin that when he peeled onions the tenants in the adjacent unit cried.

Belle enjoyed screening tenants who wanted to rent an apartment. In one instance, however, she made a mistake when she asked the applicant if he had any children.

"Six." the applicant said, "All at the cemetery."

"That's better than at Edbelle Manor," Belle thought as she continued with the screening process.

In due time the children returned from the cemetery where they were visiting the graves of relatives.

Another time an elderly man who had a long beard but wasn't particularly jolly wanted to rent an apartment. He didn't have a twinkle in his eye or a suit of red but his personality was charming as Belle was filling out the application form and said, "What is your present address?"

"Just a minute and I'll ask my girlfriend," the elderly man said.

The next question Belle asked was, "Where are you living now?"

"We sleep with relatives."

"Do you have any pets?"

"Why? Are pets necessary in order to get an apartment these days?"

"What price range are you looking for?"

"I want a one bedroom apartment in the price range of a two bedroom."

"Where are you employed?"

"At the *York Hotel.*"

"In what capacity?"

"Hold on a moment. I'll ask my girlfriend. Hey, Rosie! What is the capacity of the Hotel?"

"Over 100 drums of draft beer each month," Rosie, sitting nearby, replied.

Belle's next question was, "What is your approximate yearly income?"

"I don't know. I've been working at the hotel seven months."

"Is your girlfriend going to live with you?"

"Yes."

"How old is she?"

"Fifty eight,"

"And how old are you?"

"Sixty five,"

"And I assume you don't want your names posted on the intercom?"

The prospect said, "Yes," again.

While taking the elderly man and his girlfriend through the fourth floor unit, Belle finally asked, "Well, what do you think?"

"I think living up so high one will never have to worry about floods," the prospect replied and rented the unit.

An hour later Belle was showing a two-bedroom unit to prospective tenants and asking the usual questions: "Professionally employed?"

"We're a military family," the wife answered.

"Children?"

"Yes, nine and twelve,"

"Animals?"

"Oh, no, the children are well behaved."

Every so often Belle reviewed her tenant Credit Bureau check list and noticed that the tenant in:

- # 3 As a youngster worked on a chicken farm shovelling manure, cleaning the chicken coop and plucking chickens, 10 at a time.
- #7 At times used a trap door in the kitchen floor as a bathroom.
- #09 Always concerned about Global warming.
- #12 Had hidden Premier Manning's teleprompter before he was scheduled to make an important speech on health care.
- #14 At age 54 still wore her bikini instead of conventional clothing.
- #16 Had false teeth by the time she was eighteen.
- #19 Won a Carites Hospital Raffle and kept her money under the mattress.
- #21 Thought he was the angel of the Tar Sands.
- #22 Shouted, ``Booooo! `` Whenever royalty visited Edmonton.

#24 Thought Wal-Mart employees should be unionized.

If there ever is going to be an Apartment Caretaker's Hall Of Fame Belle Winter Bike should be the first to be inducted.

One can't possibly understand the frustration this courageous, unappreciated landlady goes through, especially when it comes to showing suites to prospective tenants. Often her side of the conversation goes something like this:

"This is a bachelor unit. Occupancy by more than one person is dangerous and unlawful. A tenant who violates an Edbelle rule will be evicted and prosecuted if necessary.

"No motorized vehicles are permitted inside. Bicycles and skateboards are allowed provided the tenant carries them through the lobby and hallway.

"Pets? Cats are allowed provided they are neutered or spade and two at the most. More than two cats and you move out, the cats may be gone but their funk lingers on. We do not allow dogs, snakes or elephants. Dogs aren't allowed because they like to relieve themselves frequently, can jump as high as the ceiling thus disturbing tenants below. Dogs also chew fixtures, electrical cords and tunnel under the door. They also carry fleas that like an in-law who moves into your basement, can be hard to kill with anything short of tactical weapons.

"This is a living room. Tenants are to use only small nails to hang pictures, clocks, calendars or *Playboy* centrefolds on. Please, no spikes, screws or bolts.

When you leave I don't want any walls to resemble a dartboard. And please don't use bleach to clean the carpet. Bleach stains things.

"Drapes? Use only proper drapes. No garbage bags, bed sheets, flags or other material with obscene pictures or words on them.

"This is the kitchen with a fridge and stove. Please keep the stove oven and elements clean. If the oven isn't cleaned regularly it may catch on fire. A fire could destroy Edbelle Manor. In the event of a fire you'll be lucky if you escape.

"This is a storage room. You may store your tires in it but please do not use it for storing green-coloured plants. And, oh, yes, never disconnect the smoke detector, which you'll find strategically located in the kitchen and hallway.

"This is the bedroom. A bedroom is a special place. A messy bedroom is unhealthy. People can't breathe in a messy room. You may install a TV or a mirror on the ceiling if you wish.

"This is the bathroom. Do not plug the toilet with foreign objects. And this is a shower curtain rod. Do not use the rod to perform a physical exercise which may give you back pain. Wash the tiles at least once a month so that mushrooms don't start sprouting.

"Finally, this is the balcony. A balcony is a place to relax at after a hard days work. Do not fling cigarette butts or buckets of water should someone give you a hard time below."

Belle also kept a journal which would help her to plan for the future. Here is a copy what she wrote for the month of November 1957.

Date November 1957 | Comment

1. Yesterday Halloween—72 kids knock on door trick or treating
2. At All Saints day yesterday I light a candle on grannies grave
3. Winter is here—Purchase a new parka at the Bay
4. Fool moon tonight—tenant in #11 expects a baby
5. A bus-sized meteor nearly missed Planet Earth yesterday
6. On TV watch the Toronto Maple Leafs against Montreal Canadiens
7. Purchase a computer—acquire Internet
8. Mike's birthday—enjoy dinner with MIKE at the Old Spaghetti Factory
9. Premier Manning visits friends at Edbelle Manor
10. Buy a red Legion poppy and pin it on jacket
11. Eleventh month of the year, eleven day of the week, eleventh hour the day. Attend Armistice Day at the cenotaph
12. Ed gives me a few hints how to use the internet
13. I'm in a dilemma if to evict tenant 14 or to give him a warning
14. My heart is broken when a drunk driver hits # 16 while crossing Jasper Avenue
15. Two years as a landlord. I'm at a crossroads if to continue as an Edbelle manager or not

16. I receive an invitation from Ed that we take holiday in Mexico and learn how to build sand castles. I'm fired up
17. Worrying if there's enough money in my back account to make a payment on the computer I purchased recently
18. Tenant # 21 makes lot of waves about the unclean condition of the laundry room
19. On the CBC channel I watch the initial program *Front Page Challenge*
20. Tenant in #7 says she grew an orchid which will bloom for four years
21. Must be getting dementia as I forgot to put out garbage for city pickup
22. So windy that a spruce tree is uprooted across the street
23. City election and I forgot to vote
24. Have spare time to read Farley Mowat's book, *The Dog Who Wouldn't Be*
25. New York Islanders in town—get Mike Bossy's autograph
26. Ed says there are more impotent things than hockey
27. Tenant in # 17 buys a 1957 Chevy
28. Tenant in # 21 says she saw a mouse on her bed—It's not a mouse but a giant bedbug
29. Tenant in #25 gives notice and will be moving to Barry, Ontario
30. Forecast for tomorrow—30 Celsius

As soon as Belle reviewed the November chronicle she received a letter from a prospective tenant whose husband was about to be transferred from Vancouver to Edmonton. Mary Wells wanted to know if a one-bedroom apartment would be available for September 1st and if a declawed cat, Blackie, was allowed to live in Edbelle Manor.

Belle wrote back:

> Dear Mrs, Wells:
>
> Yes, Edbelle Manor will have a one bedroom apartment available for September 1st and your cat, Blackie, is allowed to stay provided it is spayed or neutered and has received its vaccination shots. Personally, I think it is cruel to declaw cats, leaving them tied up and defenceless outside.
>
> Life is a lot more than a perfectly manicured lawn. Nature, in her wisdom, included cat doo-doos along with grass, rocks, trees, stars and other animals, as an essential and an integral part of Planet Earth.
>
> Since I have taken over as manager of EdBelle Manor, I did not have to call 911 or evict a cat for causing a disturbance, for abusing a spouse, using an abusive substance or language.
>
> Never in my tenure as an apartment manager have I seen or heard about a cat

kicking-in a door or wall, leave cigarette burns on the carpet, a lino or kitchen counter. Never has a cat pulled a fire alarm in the middle of the night, set a bed on fire or plugged a toilet with foreign objects.

PS: If Blackie can vouch for you and your husband, the three of you are welcome to stay at Edbelle Manor.

Yours truly,
Belle Winter-Bike
Edbelle Manor manager

A week after the Well's moved into Edbelle Manor their cat, Blackie, gave 911 a new meaning when he dialled police to help snag Herbie, the canary bird.

Mrs. Wells woke to the urgent knocking of two police constables on her door at 6:00 a.m.

The constables wanted to know what the emergency was.

"There is no emergency," Mrs. Wells said. "There must have been a mistake."

"There is no mistake, madam. The 911 emergency call was made from your apartment the first constables said and then checked the automatic dialling telephone and found a pre-programmed button for 911. When the investigation was completed the second constable said, "Elementary, my dear Mrs. Wells. Your cat, Blackie, had developed an early morning taste for a canary and had been jumping up and down trying to scoff Herbie in a cage hanging from the ceiling. In the process Blackie managed to paw 911. Case closed."

The following month Belle decided to review her September Diary, which would assist her in future planning. Belle began reading the diary with enthusiasm.

DATE IN SEPTEMBER 1958 HIGHLIGHT

1. Tenant in #11 says she can't pay her rent on time because her pay cheque was spent on her son's education. The tenant had given her occupation as a financial consultant.
2. Tenant in #19 complains that tenant in #18 is smoking marijuana. I check. It isn't marijuana but sweetgrass as part of an Indian religious ceremony.
3. A group of young people hung around Edbelle Manor who thought it sport to urinate in hallways, crush cigarettes in the carpets and paint graffiti on flat surfaces.
4. Extra fun apparently was jumping to smash light fixtures leaving hallways in total darkness for several tenants who dared to venture from their apartments after 9:00 p. m.
5. Labour Day. Trees in full colour, some so brilliant that I couldn't find one in a Crayola crayon package.
6. I find crayon and pencil marks on hallway walls. School starts tomorrow.
7. On television watch commercials with a story in the middle. Commercials more interesting than the story.
8. First frost of the season. Repair water lines into building before it snows.

9. Blustery in the morning. Rake leaves in the afternoon.
10. Tenant in #26 grows pumpkin on his balcony. Halloween soon.
Child in #26 has pumpkin seed lodged in her throat. Tenant has no phone so asks me to dial 911.
11. A harvest full moon last night. Wives of two tenants have babies overnight.
Tenant in #23 kills mouse near the entrance to Edbelle Manor using a slingshot.
12. Receive a letter from prospective tenant in Vancouver. Tenant wants to live in a community that's as exciting as Edmonton when the hockey season starts.
13. Time to paint #21. Walls had been painted with so many coats of oil base paint, 15 in all, that they have the glossy brilliance of a mirror.
14. Tenant in # 15 says he lost his keys. I give him a new set but charge $5 per key.
15. Tenant says she saw a mouse in her apartment. I hand her a Super Glue mouse/insect catcher. An hour later tenant says she was unable to catch the mouse but an unusual thing happened. The tenant's budgie bird landed in the trap and lost all its feathers while attempting to get free.
16. I wrote a column for the *Journal* but the editor says I need to improve my spelling.
17. Find time to read about Terry Fox, humanitarian, athlete and cancer treatment activist.
18. Tenant in #25 says it's going to snow because his arthritis is bothering him.

19. Tenant in #11 complains about the high cost of pills he's taking. I suggest she contact the local Member of Parliament Les "Speed" Westgate.
20. Tenant in #12 becomes a Canadian citizen. I celebrate the occasion with her enjoying a cup herbal tea and cookies.
21. Autumn begins. Days get shorter. Electric bills will be higher.
22. Three inches of snow falls on Edmonton overnight. Roads slippery.
23. Kids playing street hockey in back alley break basement window of #02
24. Tenant in #05 says she saw a UFO flying towards Vancouver.
25. Welfare, Canada Pension and Old Age Security cheques arrive today.
26. Chamber of Commerce survey indicate that Edmonton's population, because of the oil boom, may reach 2 million by the year 2098 at which time the city may decide to hold a referendum if to break away from the rest of Canada.
27. Edmonton experiencing Indian summer. Hunting season opens.
28. Evict tenant in #10. The tenant says I'm an *asshole* and threatens me with a hockey stick. Street hockey is very popular at this time of the year.
29. Tenant in #14 has car stolen.
30. Attend exhibition hockey game between Edmonton Oilers and Calgary Flames
31. Edmonton Eskimos loose 26-15 to Saskatchewan Roughriders

Although Belle was a shrewd businesswoman she was also compassionate. The compassion occurred when a couple applied for a one-bedroom apartment and were up front when each said they had just been released from prison after serving an eight-year sentence for committing a major robbery.

"We have served our time and need a break so we can get on with our lives." the male ex-prisoner said.

"We realize that as a landlord it's a difficult decision for you to make based on our past, but please accept us as tenants. We won't let you down," the female companion continued.

"But how do you propose to pay for the rent and security deposit?" Belle asked the couple and both indicated they were on Social Assistance during a rehabilitation period and the rent would be paid as a third party directly to the landlord.

Belle wasn't certain that Providence would find her better tenants so she gambled and said, "Okay, I'll accept both of you as tenants."

An Application and an Occupancy Contract were signed, an In/Out report done and since that time the former prison inmates became two of the better tenants Edbelle Manor ever had.

This was not the case, however, with another tenant, who was released from jail and after he moved in called 911. Thirty seconds later he changed his mind and said to the police, "Do not come to my apartment in Edbelle Manor."

This particular tenant was later shot at by police who stormed his basement apartment after he stabbed one of the policemen with a rusty jackknife.

Following the Police Policy Manuel the two cops followed up the 911 calls even after it was cancelled. They knocked on the occupant's door but nobody answered.

As the two officers were walking up a flight of stairs, the tenant emerged from his apartment, lunged at one of the officers and stabbed him in the shoulder. The tenant then barricaded himself inside his apartment.

The officers called for reinforcements, including the tactical squad but before the SWAT arrived, the two officers at the scene rushed the apartment. The tenant again lunged at one of the officers and they shot him twice in the abdomen.

Edmonton police would not say why the officers entered the tenant's apartment before the tactical squad arrived but Belle felt SWAT members had better equipment and are trained to deal with similar situations, one of which occurred the following day when Belle bopped an intruder on the head with a baseball bat.

This followed numerous break-and-enters in the neighbourhood and a suspicious looking stranger entered Edbelle Manor.

"I have reached the end of my rope. I have exhausted every avenue with the police department. I didn't know what to do. I just wanted to subdue the intruder," Belle said to Ed when he questioned her about being charged with assault with a deadly weapon.

Belle described how she waited for the intruder at the bottom of the stairs at the front entrance. "I had the bat down by my legs when this creep stopped and said, 'Oh, you are going to hit me with that, eh?' Then he came down at me swinging, I grabbed the intruder by the neck with my left hand and with my right I bopped him with the bat with all my strength."

Belle said she didn't call police because, "Due to recent cutbacks, I didn't think they would respond. All I wanted to do is protect my tenants."

As it turned out Belle did not call the police but a tenant did. Two officers arrived and after reviewing the incident arrested the intruder who had 28 outstanding warrants for his arrest and more aliases than Belle had shoes.

The month of December was exiting but stressful for Belle. Her monthly diary read as follows:

<u>Date In December 1960 Comment</u>

1. Time to decorate the lobby with a Christmas tree, strings of lights, and wreath on the entrance door. Hang icicles and snowflakes from the ceiling. Spray frost on the windows. Tenants already humming, 'I'm Dreaming of a White Christmas'. Ho, ho, ho spoken here. Tenant in # 4 says the first thing at Christmas that pains her is sending Christmas cards and the second, her husband rigging up the balcony lights.

2. During a storm two feet of snow falls overnight on Edmonton. Snowmen dance all night while I shovelled snow off sidewalks and the roof. So cold outside you can hear your breath. Too cold to kiss. Too cold to think. Edbelle heating system breaks down.
3. I figure out that to deliver his gifts in one night Santa would have to make 822.6 visits per second, sleighing at 3000 times the speed of sound. At that speed Santa and his reindeer would burst into fames instantaneously.
   Tenant in #11 loses mailbox key. Expects a Pavarotti album from Italy.
4. Cleaning lady wins $500 at a Minor Hockey Christmas Raffle
5. Tenants and I are looking forward to Christmas.
6. Big pre-Christmas sale at Wal-Mart. Many TV Specials at the Brick.
7. Fifteen shopping days until Christmas
8. Tenant in #2 wants a snowmobile for Christmas
9. Tenant in #3 wants a shotgun so he can quiet down his neighbour.
10. Donate to the Salvation Army.
11. Rumour spreads that Christmas and Chanukah will merge next year. Donner and Blitzen will retire but not Rudolph.
12. I notice tenant in # 23 keeps more beer than food in his fridge.
13. Tenant in #22 says he earns $40,000 but can't afford to buy Christmas presents. He also plays rock n roll music at three in the morning.

14. Postman begins Christmas deliveries to Edbelle tenants. Tenant in #26 receives a partridge in a pear tree. Two turtledoves are delivered to #14, three French hens (I assume to be turned into Kentucky fried chicken) to # 12 and four Calling Birds (Noisy little things) to # 04.
15. What a surprise. Postman delivers five golden rings to #7. Frankly the squawking birds are beginning to get on my nerves.
16. Postman is back to the birds again. Delivers six huge geese to # 21, seven a-laying swans to # 8. Some tenants are complaining about the birds and their eggs. "There's also bird doo-doo all over Edbelle Manor, the stairway, hallways and even the lobby and the birds are squawking all night," other tenants complain. I'm a nervous wreck.
17. On this day the postman makes a special delivery of eight maids who milk eight cows in unit 19. I still don't know how the tenant found room for an additional eight maids (cuties) and eight cows (Holsteins) in his bachelor unit. I do know however, the cows were dancing and the maids singing *Jingle Bells* in the hallways during the middle of the night thus causing a disturbance. Cops arrive but after noticing the cows had diarrhoea, left. I can't sleep at nights.
18. I hear nine pipers playing in the lobby. They never stopped chasing those maids since morning. The cows are upset and are stepping all over the screeching birds. Feathers all over. Tenant in # 5 starts a petition to fire me. I say, "You'll get yours."

19. I watch ten Lords visiting tenant in unit #25, and leaping out of the second floor balcony. I find all the birds dead. A major health problem exists.
20. Twelve marching drummers arrived at Edbelle Manor with the Health Inspector, who after a thorough inspection says "Mrs. Remus, you have 24-hours to clean up or else I'll condemn the building."
    I do as I'm told. Christmas Eve is around the corner.
21. Take part in a last midnight shopping spree and then suggest to Ed the Midnight Madness should be made into an Olympic Event.
22. Get hair done where the hairdresser plays her favourite Christmas song in the background, 'Oh, Comb All Ye faithful'.
23. Christmas Eve. Mike and I attend a midnight service at the No Name Universal Church. Mike and I eat a bucket of chicken wings, many cookies and glasses of eggnog. At 3:00 a.m. I hang a pair of my pantyhose over the fireplace.
24. Christmas day—Mike and I open our Christmas presents. Ed got a pair of black socks and a beautiful necktie to match is eyes.
    I didn't get anything because Santa's note said my pantyhose had a hole in it. Ed and I enjoy a turkey dinner. Argue over wishbone.
25. Boxing Day. Watch a TV replay of the 1951 heavyweight boxing match between Joe Louis and Rocky Marciano.
26. Tenant in # 23 complains that second hand smoke from Santa's pipe is affecting her health.

27. Learned from Santa, which tenant is naughty and which one is nice. Whenever you are at a loss for words say "Ho, Ho, Ho." Never pout and a bright red coat can make anyone look good.
28. On this date nothing fits me, not even my blouse. The cookies I nibbled, the eggnog I drank at holiday parties had gone to my waist
30. A postman with a hernia shows up with a sack full of bills. He's whistling and shouting as he calls out their names: "Mrs Summer. Here's one from Super Store. This one from the Bay! Here's one from Canada Tire.

And hey, one from Visa! Another from Master Charge and still another from American Express. To the top of your limit, you shopped at every mall, you've charged away—charged away all!"

Ed and I get ready for the New Years Ball at the Westin Hotel to usher in New Year and make resolutions: To eat more, put on weight, start smoking, quit exercising and through all this sing *Auld Lang Syne*.

The night feels like a chilly Halloween as revellers dressed in top hats and feather boas stroll past the snow banks to the hotel while Mike and I watch through the main window the fireworks at Churchill Square and enjoy a glass of champaign at the same time.

The following night Belle was halfway through her security inspection when a tall male stranger with a skull tattoo on his chest and an ugly nose pitted with blackheads, a face deeply scared from acne and long black waxy hair flopping over his face, walked up to her and suspiciously said, "Good morning, Mam. Can you spare me a cigarette?"

"And who are you?" Belle said.

"I'm a visitor.

"Is that so?" Belle said pointing to a sign posted near the entrance door, which read *No Visitors after 11:00 P. M.* "Who are you visiting?"

"A friend."

"Who's your friend?" Belle said but thought she already knew.

"I can't tell."

"Is it Debbie Buggy in apartment 04?"

"I guess so."

"Now that we have established who you are visiting, I'll tell you something."

"What?"

"I want you to leave this building within five minutes or else I'll call the cops."

"Okay. Okay. I'll leave."

An hour had passed before Belle knocked on Ms Buggy's door wanting to confirm that the visitor had left.

"He certainly has." Mrs. Buggy said and slammed the door in Belle's face.

Belle thought Ms Buggy was harbouring the criminal so she called police and when two officers arrived ran Ms Buggy's name through a computer which showed there was an outstanding warrant for her arrest for failing to appear in Court on a previous charge.

The stranger was found hiding in the bedroom closet and when his name was ran through the same computer, it was found that the stranger had a Canada-wide warrant for his arrest for escaping a prison. The computer showed that the stranger, years ago, at a For Sale by Owner home murdered a woman, had the body chopped into pieces and thrown into a garbage dumpster in a back alley.

The home was eventually sold but the bride and groom who purchased it at the time felt the murder should have been disclosed when they purchased the house but it wasn't.

As for Ms Buggy she posted a bond and was out of jail the same evening. Ms Buggy wasn't surprised when Belle handed her an eviction notice. As for the stranger he was returned to prison.

As soon as Ms Buggy's apartment was vacant Belle hired a plumber to replace a damaged sink. While the plumber was working Belle met Ed for lunch. When she returned, an hour later, the plumber was still working.

"How is it going?" Belle said.

"Fine, just fine," the plumber replied. "Since I saw you last the basement at Edbelle Manor has turned into a swimming pool."

"I can't believe it," Belle said after seeing the knee-deep water in the basement and phoned Edmonton Emergency Control and Carpet Cleaning

When the van arrived, the operator unpacked a long vacuum hose, sucked up the water and then steamed cleaned the carpets.

As soon as the operator left, the plumber said he was unable to remove the sink because the vacuum operator had sucked up his screwdriver and would Belle bring him another one.

Belle, more familiar with spirits than with tools, brought the plumber a glass, a can of orange juice and a bottle of vodka, placed them on the kitchen counter and disappeared.

By 5:00 p. m. the plumber got slightly inebriated and instead of working overtime or going home, climbed into the Edbelle Manor attic and fell asleep not noticing the bats hanging from the rafters.

For three consecutive days the plumber did not show up for work. Thinking that he had quit Belle decided to do the plumbing herself. As she was installing a new sink she noticed a strange odour coming from the direction of the attic.

She had never smelled anything like this before so she grabbed a ladder, opened the door leading to the attic barely squeezing herself inside, and probed with a flashlight.

Belle already knew there were bats inside the attic but was surprised that the plumber was inside also and did not breathe. "What the H is going on here? There's no use resuscitating him," Belle said to herself and immediately phoned police but the policeman who answered the phone argued that it wasn't in the *Police Policy Manual* to determine if a person is dead or alive. "It's the work of the coroner," the policeman said.

When Belle phoned the coroner's office she was told that the coroner was about to strike for higher wages and was working rule to rule.

It was another three days before the coroner did arrive to view the body but in that time, the bats had their *Last Supper* and devoured the plumber. An inquest or as a matter of fact, an autopsy, wasn't necessary.

The coroner reported the death as SPDS—Sudden Plumbers Death Syndrome. This is a syndrome of unexplained death among plumbers who ingest screwdrivers while at work.

The report was unchallenged except by hundreds of bats that swarmed out of the attic and dropped dead in the middle of the parking lot. Like the plumber the bats decided to die. There were no last words.

Belle never did find out what actually caused the bats to suddenly commit a mass suicide but said, "Maybe the bats belonged to a cult."

Secretly she wished the same happened to some of her tenants.

During a February night that the bats died there was a full moon, a time when strange things usually happen in Edmonton and no vandal in sight. It was a time too when earlier in the day many of the Edbelle Manor tenants received their welfare cheques and bars, bingo halls and streets were filled with people.

Police, firemen and ambulance paramedics were to busy to answer a phone call placed by an Edbelle tenant. That night there was a huge explosion at Edbelle Manor and a fire and smoke that followed destroyed Mike's first revenue producing property.

A Fire Marshall's report showed that a tenant in apartment #05, Mrs. Raunchy, had found a cockroach in the bathroom so she picked up a tissue and tossed the insect into the toilet bowl.

Seeing that the roach was still moving the tenant took a can of insect repellent and sprayed the bowl making certain the roach was dead. What happened next in 1961 Edmonton will never forget.

Five minutes later Mrs. Raunchy had to go to the bathroom and while doing her thing, tossed a cigarette butt into the toilet bowl.

The cigarette made contact with the repellent causing a huge explosion followed by a fire. Mrs. Raunchy was found dead and her friend in the adjacent apartment was severely injured.

A week later the daughter buried Mrs. Raunchy in a cemetery and bought several packages of carnations to decorate the grave. The daughter was so upset with her mother's tragedy that she took the first flight available to a Mexican resort to pull herself together. When she returned doo doo hit the fan at the Home Depot complaint department.

It seems when the daughter returned home and visited the cemetery where her mother's grave was completely covered with, not carnations but rhubarb.

Mind you she could have been the first in the neighbourhood to enjoy rhubarb pie and coffee but she was so upset and shaking so much that she couldn't lift a pie plate.

As for Mike Bike he diversified. With insurance covering Edbelle Manor he used the thousands of dollar windfall to make down payments on other revenue properties.

Mike was 31 years old and Bike Manor, Bike Place, Bike Square, Bike Centre, Bike Row, Bike Plaza, Bike Village and Bike Tower were visible projects across Canada. Not bad for a young man whose father was an immigrant and years ago drove a dray truck for $3.00 an hour,

As for Belle she now had the experience of being a landlord and accepted an offer from the *Journal* to write a daily column on landlord/tenant relationships. Her first column dealt with *top ten* silly questions prospective tenants asked while applying at Edbelle Manor.

1. How far is the nearest shopping mall?
2. Can we practice lawn bowling in the hallway?
3. When does a cockroach become a lobster?
4. Are their fish in the North Saskatchewan River?
5. Is the bedroom large enough for a king-size bed?
6. Have you any Amish hookers as tenants?
7. What is the official language at Edbelle Manor?
8. Can I borrow a ten until my welfare cheque arrives?
9. Can I photocopy a set of keys?
10. February has 28 days. What other months have 28 days?

Belle's second column listed Ten Good Reasons Not to Be an Apartment Manager

1. You are in a job that humiliates you and the least thing you want is to be sarcastic while collecting rents.

2. Your job is about to be rendered obsolete by some exciting new-cost cutting technology
3. Your tenants are harassing you and calling you dirty names.
4. You are in the middle of a management change.
5. Separates husband and wife in leading a normal wife.
6. An arsonist may burn the building down.
7. Managing an apartment building isn't good for your health.
8. When you leave the apartment there are tenants who will never forget you.
9. You won't get a good night's sleep as someone always rings the wrong buzzer.
10. Once you manage an apartment building you may then decided to enter politics.

Belle's third column listed Ten Tips for being a Successful Landlord

1. Don't rent to anyone before checking his/her credit history
2. Get all the important terms of the tenancy in writing. Beginning with the rental application and lease or rental agreement.
3. Establish a clear, fair system of collecting, holding and returning security deposits.
4. Stay on top of repair and maintenance needs and make repairs requested promptly
5. Don't let your tenants and property be easy marks for a criminal. You could be liable for the tenant's losses.
6. Respect your tenants' privacy. Notify tenants whenever you plan to enter their rental suite.

7. Disclose environmental hazards such as lead and asbestos.
8. Purchase enough liability and other property insurance.
9. Try to resolve disputes with tenants without lawyers and lawsuits.
10. Make certain you do an In/Out Report as soon as the tenant moves in.

Belle's fourth column dealt with her Edbelle Manor diary for the month of February. This column was twice as long as the other.

<u>Dated February 1961</u> <u>Highlight</u>

1. Cat in #22 falls off second balcony but isn't hurt because of a five-foot snow bank.
2. Groundhog Day. Six more weeks of winter.
3. Tenant in #25 says she was ripped off when washing machine in laundry didn't work.
4. Tenant in #03 says she has developed cabin fever.
5. Tenant in #20 has difficulty starting his pickup. He fiddles with the carburetor. I lend him my jumping cables.
6. Tenant in #10 leaves window wide open overnight. Heating pipe burst because they got frozen. Water flowing from third floor to basement. I call a carpet cleaner and plumber. Damage estimated at $2000.
7. I read in the papers that Elvis Presley is promoted to a sergeant in the U. S. army.

8. Tenant in #17 asks if she can install a deadbolt on her door. Says a character with a long black beard seen prowling the hallway after midnight.
9. City inspector says to clear snow off sidewalk in front of Edbelle Manor.
10. A transient found sleeping in the dumpster and is half-frozen. Transient says he fell asleep while collecting beer/pop bottles and cans.
11. Tenants in #16 and #07 have bowling competition in the hallway by using empty beer bottles and a cantaloupe.
12. Another snowstorm hits Edmonton I shovel snow from the sidewalk. Snowplough comes and I shovel the same snow a second time. I get back pain.
13. I visit Dr. Hardy and he says while shovelling snow I should used the rhythm method.
14. It's Valentine's Day. A card and chocolates from Mike.
15. Still have back pain but Doc Hardy says not to have sex the rhythm method but I should have shovelled the snow with a rhythm. One, two, shovel.
16. Tenant in #19 has toilet trouble leaving plunger upright. In the middle of the night doesn't switch on the light and finds plunger handle halfway up her rectum.
17. Snowplough driver asks for permission to canvas Edbelle Manor so he can sell Minor Hockey tickets.
18. Cleaning lady phones and says she can't come to work because there's a deer stuck in her porch entrance.

19. By now I have a love/hate relationship with Edbelle Manor. I hate to get there in the morning and love to leave in the evening so I can be with Ed.
20. A paper airplane from the third floor balcony hits tenant below. Tenant angry.
21. Cleaning lady has the flu.
22. Overnight the water in the toilet of #03 turns to ice. I phone the plumber and he says to me, "Please place a sign outside that reads, *Don't Eat Brown Snow*.
23. I hand the law to tenant in #08 and say to him, 'I'll give you two days to pay your rent' and he says to me 'Two days. Okay. How about July1st and Christmas?'
24. Was going to go ice-fishing with Mike but our worms were frozen so hard that we didn't want the fish to break their teeth.
25. Tenant in #13 says she heard a robin chirping. I say to her, "You would be chirping too if you were covered with three feet of snow."
26. Tenant in #12 asks if I can help her fill out her income tax form.
27. Snow begins melting. Tenant in #04 sets up a hibachi in the hallway.
28. Edbelle destroyed by an explosion and a fire that followed.
29. Leap year.

CHAPTER 4

It was in the early 60's that there were times when Mike called on those who purchased properties through him and also on knowledgeable people to help evaluate possible listings. For instance, one day Mike met with Pastor Taylor and farmer Jerry Fix at a spot overlooking a cliff with a panoramic view. Looking towards the magnificent view Mike said, "An ideal location to build a luxury hotel, don't you think?"

Reverend Taylor put on his glasses, took a long look at the view and then shaking his head said, "I wouldn't disturb a speck of dirt here. This piece of land is a masterpiece created by God."

What farmer Fix said was, "This particular piece of land is a hole in which I wouldn't want my horses or cows die in."

The following day Mike had difficulty appraising a religious estate so he invited Father McCarthy, Reverend Taylor and Rabbi Libowitch to come along and help determine how much the property was worth.

As the four men arrived at the estate they were horrified to see through a lit and an uncurtained window a man and a woman were in a compromising position.

After a careful look inside Father McCarthy decided the offending couple was not of the Catholic faith.

"How did you reach that conclusion?" Mike asked.

"Simple. There's no crucifix on the wall."

Reverend Taylor also took a look and he too declared the couple was not of his flock.

"How do you know?" Mike said.

"There's no *Bible* on the shelf."

It was Rabbi Libowtich's turn to look and when he did, returned with a look of shame and said, "It's one of us."

"How do you know?" Mike asked again.

"Simple," the rabbi said, "The wall-to-wall carpets."

A farmer who purchased a 160 acre farm through Ed in the Cry Baby district was a chronic complainer. For years this farmer complained that the weather had been against him, insects had eaten what little crop he grew and always the market was low when he was ready to sell.

The following year there was a bumper crop and was selling wheat at above average prices and exporting out of the country so Mike casually said, "Well, you really made it big this year."

"Fair, just fair." the farmer replied. "Besides, a harvest like that is hard on the soil."

Sometimes one can't win.

After Mike had spoken to this particular farmer he had an appointment with a well-dressed man wearing dark glasses who identified himself as the chief executive officer of a major construction company wishing to build a gigantic shopping mall in Edmonton. Mike had doubts this man was a CEO not because of how he dressed but by what he said, "Our company motto is to buy dirt cheap and sell at the highest market."

"You obviously haven't bought top soil lately." Mike thought but used good judgement and instead asked the man to describe the proposed mall.

"Well, *West Edmonton Mall* is huge but the one our company is proposing is bigger still. It will be so big that we are thinking of air conditioning the forest within the mall and the property will be glassed in."

"Wow!" Mike exclaimed. "That will be quite a shopping mall."

"It will be with each component being the largest in the world. The mall will be a world within a world and its appeal will be its scale and the mythology. Like Mount Everest it will attract more people than *West Edmonton Mall* because it will be the biggest mall on Planet Earth."

Despite the hype the mall never did get off the ground. Instead one was built in Dubai, United Arab Emirates.

Real estate agencies as a rule hold their sales meeting on a Monday morning. Following the meeting salesmen climb into cars and tour properties, which were listed during the week. Since his marriage to Belle Mike became a salesman who made many sales and attended meetings and tours on a regular basis. Ed was a salesman who never took a rejection as a personal matter and among other things, thought of himself as exceptionally talented with attributes of an *Avon* lady and an *Electrolux* consultant. As a matter of fact Mike often referred to himself as a real estate consultant than a realtor, broker or a salesman.

By now Mike learned to study real estate trends, statistics, draw various graphs and maps.

He was persistent and had confidence in his ability to do what he wanted most—negotiate deals, become wealthy and then enter politics. "Real estate salesmen are sensitive beings and because they are easily hurt," Mike said to himself and on many occasions he was.

Mike had talent and craftsmanship and each morning while driving to work listened to motivational tapes. By now Mike also had taken courses in psychology, in negotiating skills including eye contact, body language, transience of population and numerous other subjects in order to improve his sales and personal abilities. What Mike had learned was that as a rule 20% of the salesmen do 80% of listings and volume of sales.

As soon as Very Best, Best Realty owner and agent, said, "Grab your cup of coffee as the sales meeting will start shortly." Mike and other members of the sales force filled their cups and sat in the bullpen and then Best said, "Good morning," a customary greeting.

"Good morning," the salesmen replied simultaneously.

"Item one. I trust everyone had a good weekend listing properties." Best said and gave each salesman an opportunity to say what they had accomplished over the weekend. One salesman said that he had listed Judge Black's home but warned, "Beware of the Doberman pincher the judge keeps in the basement."

Another salesman said he had listed a, "Bulldozer Special."

Another said she had listed a duplex and then gave a brief description of the property.

Mike said that he had listed a multi-bedroom split level in a gated golf community and would be delighted to show McMansion which was enormous and in a subdivision where houses were on top of each other, the owners were wealthy and Filipino maids wore Rolexes. The house was no *Buckingham Palace* or one like Canada's Prime Minister lived in, still it was luxurious and huge.

When Best spoke again he said, "Item two. The *Royal Bank* has lowered its interest rate by one-half percent. Other banks are expected to follow in lowering mortgage rates too."

Best then pointed to a blackboard at the side of the room, which recorded sales completions and new listings. Pointing his finger towards Ed he then said, "Mike, how many deals have you completed this month."

"Twenty-one and another seven are pending."

"Good. Good," Best said, "Salesmen, tell your clients to purchase now. The price won't get much better. Item three—advertising. Is Best Realty advertising effective?"

Mike raised his hand.

"Okay, Mike, go ahead."

What Mike said was that he had 10 calls inquiring about a lot advertised in the local papers and wondered what the callers were talking about. On checking, however, he found the newspapers had a large apartment listed with the lot write-up the pictures did not match.

"Even I would pay $5000 for a $500,000 apartment block," Mike said.

When the meeting finished dealing with advertising Best continued, "Item four. Collapsed deals. Have we any?"

"I have one," a salesman said.

"Tell me about it."

"Well, I sold a piece of vacant land but now the purchaser wants his money back."

"Reason?"

"Because the Water District will provide water to only one-half of the land."

"Was the subject to clause removed?"

"It was and the purchaser checked with governing authorities."

"Well, Best Realty is a stakeholder as far as the deposit is concerned. Get in touch with the vendor and see to it that no feathers are ruffled."

When salesmen finished discussing, "Collapsed Deals" Best continued, "Item five, Commercial Properties."

Mike said he had listed several commercial properties, which he personally made an offer on them.

After salesmen dealt with Commercial Properties Best said, "Item six. Open Houses. Who held an Open House over the weekend?"

Several hands were raised including Mike's who said he had two Open Houses going between 2:00 and 5:00 in the afternoon. Mike said that on Saturday howls of pain emerged from the bathroom when Nike found a prospective buyer glued to a toilet seat. An ambulance crew managed to pry the prospect from the seat, which had been covered with glue by practical jokers that had passed through the house earlier.

"And the Open House you held on Sunday. What happened?".

"Following the Open House on Sunday I had a black eye and some explaining to do to Belle."

"What happened?"

"It happened when I coughed."

"When you coughed? I don't believe it."

"Believe it," Mike said, "It happened as I was examining the bedroom closet and the owner thought I was in love with his wife but I wasn't."

Best then handed each salesman a list of tips on preparing Open Houses. The tip note read: "Here Are 10 Tips to Remember While Preparing Your Open House." Tidy your home. Dirty laundry/dishes are a definite no-no.

1. Use air fresheners throughout the home. Contact a Chinese herbalist for the aroma of your choice.
2. Unclutter your cupboards and closets.
3. Shovel your sidewalks in winter. Manicure your lawn in summer. In both cases make certain no doggy doo-doo is in sight.
4. Make minor repairs. Leaky faucets, torn wallpaper or broken windows can make or break a sale.
5. Turn all the lights on and play soft instrumental music in the background.
6. Put valuables away including *Krazy Glue* which a looky loo may put on top of a toilet cover.
7. If Open House is slow the salesperson can catch up on reading or knitting.
8. If you have a family pet take it with you.

"Remember—first impressions are lasting impressions. Make certain the salesman is wearing black socks/pantyhose.
PS: Imagine an agent trying to explain to a potential purchaser who has just slipped and fallen that your Open House is truly the home for him."

Following the meeting, as part of the ritual of property familiarization, salesmen hopped into cars and toured listings they discussed at the meeting just concluded.

As a group the salesmen first toured Judge Black's home. When it was confirmed that an angry Doberman was tied up in the basement Mike's comment was, "If a judge is so cruel to an animal, how can he give proper sentences to people?"

At the McMansion home in the gated golf community, Mike thought he would have some fun by doing a trick on his co-salesmen. He hid inside an entrance closet and as the elderly salesman, Jim Crook, opened the door, Mike yelled loudly, "Boo! The ghost of McMansion is after your soul!"

Crook got so frightened that he collapsed. An ambulance took Crook to Emergency where a doctor on duty confirmed that he had a heart attack. Since that time Mike decided not to play tricks on his co-workers, especially if they were elderly.

When Mike led his group of salesmen to the master bedroom of the next home he became embarrassed and so was the couple inside lying on a bed. It seems that the vendor was at work and the wife decided to invite a male friend for mid-morning coffee. As Mike cautiously opened the bedroom door he was surprised and so was the couple as it scrambled to cover-up with blankets.

At first Mike thought the couple was husband and wife so he apologized for the intrusion but seconds later noticed a pair of pants placed on a chair had golden-coloured stripes and a cap lying next to the pants, had an emblem on it with the words *Royal Canadian Mounted Police.*

As other salesmen approached the bedroom Mike put his hand to his lips and whispered quietly, "Shhhh, this bedroom is occupied so we'll have to end our tour of this home."

"But I want to see the master bedroom" a salesman protested. mike shook his head and said, "Sorry. This is one bedroom we are unable to see as part of our tour," Mike said apologetically.

"Why?" another salesmen protested.

"Because there's a changing of the guard taking place."

"What is that supposed to mean?" another salesman asked.

"It means Mounties always get their man, if not the man, then his wife."

After tem years of marriage Belle got tired of living on acreage with a barn and two-bedroom cabin on it. The modest size cabin imposed too many limitations, especially when it came to entertaining and there was no garage. Over a cup of coffee Belle asked Mike if they could purchase another home. Mike agreed and after several viewings was prepared make an offer on one that Belle liked and asked the middle-aged woman what she thought the property was worth.

"I'm not sure what you mean," the proprietor said.

"For example, if your husband died, what do you think you'd get?"

"If my husband died?"

"Yes."

The woman thought for a second and then said, "Jim used to talk a lot so I would get a parrot."

After a fair offer was rejected Mike and Belle decided to build a second home on their acreage.

The house they built was a brick two-story four-bedroom bungalow modest in size with a garage and a swimming pool near the cabin. Both had a panoramic view of Edmonton and the North Saskatchewan River. Ed insisted that that every tree and shrub should be preserved and was surprised by the high price he had to pay for the bricks and lumber. The floor of the library was mutinously assembled from oak. The electrical circuits and plumbing hidden inside the walls were absolutely modern. The house was centrally air conditioned which was unheard of in Edmonton at the time.

The house was computerized with the finest security system, utilized satellites and silicon microchips and equipped with a sound system and a kitchen where appliances could think electronically and talk with each other. Mike also hired four permanent full time foreign workers which included Christian Palaganas from the Philippines as a house keeper whose long view intention was to become a Canadian citizen, Mustapha Khalid, a handyman/ gardener from Morocco whose intention was to become a Canadian citizen. Toto Yoshida whose intention was to become a Canadian citizen and Harjet Singh an internet graduate from NAIT and with an intention to return to India. Mike's ability to build a new and larger home, to renovate the barn and to hire four foreign contract workers at the same time said a lot about how Mike's real estate business was doing.

As soon as Mike and Belle moved into their new brick home, which was furnished with eighteenth century antiques, many attended the housewarming at which time Pastor Taylor blessed the structure and then asked Belle, "What makes you think Ed is a good Christian?"

"Well, I know he loves his enemies," Belle replied.

"That's fine. What enemies does he have?"

"His home-brewed beer."

By now Mike diversified to the point that whatever he touched turned into wealth and some even gave him the moniker Donald Trump North or a *tycoon* instead Realtor Mike. Aside from selling real estate Ed continued drinking beer and purchasing revenue-producing properties including the Fishing Hunting and Golf Resort at Cooking Lake near Edmonton. Mike made the purchase for his parents.

Mike's Vancouver acquisition included a twin-tower high-rise overlooking Stanley Park and the Pacific Ocean.

In Calgary Ed purchased another high-rise and in Edmonton various garden apartments and townhouses throughout the city.

Ed was vying unchallenged for the "Canadian Realtor Of The Year Award" and when it was announced that he was the winner, his nearest competitor, Mary Todd from RE/MAX was asked to make the presentations at a meeting of the Edmonton Real Estate Board. Ms Todd congratulated Ed on behalf of the realtors present and then asked him to say a few words about his success.

Mike Bike knew how to sell. He single-handily out performed larger offices throughout Canada. He also knew the way to stay first is to stay fast, and to stay connected.

Ed began his speech with, "Not only do I have to work faster. I also need to get my clients to react faster. Just because a transaction is done, that doesn't mean the relationship is over."

Next in a short talk Mike said, "When people think of real estate in Western Canada, they now think of Michael Bike. I have created an identity. I know that people when either buying or selling, believe in me."

"When my name pops up they think I work harder, know the market better than anyone else, fight for my clients and above all I'm honest."

While Mike was causing a sensation in the real estate industry Belle was causing havoc with the local traffic police. It seems the well-proportioned Belle was scantily garbed in shorts and a halter fertilizing the pumpkins, pulling up dandelions and crabgrass in the garden at her new residence when a patrol car stopped in front of her.

The officer got out, introduced himself and said, "Would you mind telling me how long you've been working in the garden?"

"At least an hour."

"Just as I thought," the cop said. "You see, we had a successful radar trap set up down the road. About an hour ago traffic slowed down considerably. Offhand I'd say you put us out of business."

"Good. Good," Belle replied. "My husband and I are against the use of radar traps in order to fill the city coffers."

"Just doing what we are told."

That wasn't the only time Belle got the attention of motorists. Earlier she received tulips from a friend in Holland. Belle kept asking Ed to plant the bulbs but being a busy salesman didn't find the time.

Desperately Belle planted the bulbs herself. Naturally Ed was delighted especially when the bright red flowers came up in the spring in glowing colours that proclaimed: *ED I LOVE YOU*.

In the real estate industry salesmen do a lot of advertising and deal not only with vendors and purchasers but also on occasion with animals, ghosts, tramps and clairvoyants. Take for instance the day Mike closed a "Big Deal" and he and Belle were enjoying a glass of beer at the *Best Western Hotel*. As the couple were relaxing a moose with large antlers stumbled into the bar.

Being a member of the Edmonton Moose Lodge Mike hollered, "Unbelievable! Don't anyone harm that moose!"

But what Belle did surprised everyone as she picked up Mike's jacket, which was placed on a chair and threw it towards the animal's head. The moose got frightened and ran off into a nearby forest with the jacket stuck onto his antlers.

It took several seconds before Mike realized that inside his jacket was his wallet containing credit cards, identification papers along with an offer to purchase which he was to present within an hour and where time was of the essence.

It took several hours before a summoned game warden tranquilized the moose so that Mike could recover his jacket but in that time the subject to clause with the offer had expired and Mike lost $3000 in commission.

Another time Mike was in the *Sandman Hotel* bar when, a security guard at the hotel, entered the room, had a bowl of milk and began dancing on the countertop.

"Dominic! Stop your nonsense!" the hotel manager hollered but the animal paid no attention and kept on dancing.

Annoyed by the antics the manager hollered again, "Dominic! Stop your nonsense!" but the dog kept on dancing. Finally the manager hollered a third time. Dominic you are fired!" and inserted an ad in Job Bank for a security guard, preferably a German shepherd.

Hearing the manager's loud voice patrons in the bar began talking about Dominic's intelligence.

Mike said that Dominic at one time belonged to Belle and that the dog had an I. Q. so high that he operated a computer and was the most intelligent dog in all of Edmonton, "And anyone who has a smarter dog better prove it."

"Okay." said a patron sitting next to Mike. "I have a dog which chases butterflies and drinks water out of a toilet bowl. I accept Bowser as a companion."

The story was matched by another patron who said his dog was smarter because the animal had recorded a Christmas album.

Still another patron said that his dog was even smarter and told how the dog would fetch a quart of milk and pour it into a glass. "I adore Pooch." the patron said.

"Okay." Mike finally said and called Dominic to his side and said. "Go show the guys what you can do."

Dominic made an exit and instead of going to a computer went to each patrons home and drank milk, had sex with the other dogs, claimed he injured his back, filed for Workman's Compensation benefits and went Belle's parent's farm on sick leave. Dominic being fired was no big deal.

Next day Mike went to check on a house he had sold and the purchaser complained that there was a ghost inside.

Sure enough as Mike knocked on the door a ghost began chasing him. The two ran until Mike became exhausted and stopped to sit on a log. When the ghost caught up he said to Mike, "That was quite a run we had."

The frightened Mike looked up. "And we'll have another as soon as I catch my breath."

Unexplained events occur constantly in Edmonton, particularly during the tourist season.

Events like the swimming pool suddenly draining by itself and no vandal in sight.

The psychic phenomena continued when Mike listed a house and the ghost inside invited Mike to join him reading verses from a poetry book.

As soon as they finished reading and it got dark outside the ghost walked through a wall, and Mike, trying to follow him, broke his nose and missed the next week at work.

As soon as an insurance agent heard about Mike's nose he immediately phoned and suggested that Mike take out an accident insurance policy.

"Why should I take out a policy?" Mike asked.

"Listen, Mike. Last week I sold a policy to a competitor of yours. Next day while searching for a listing, she broke her neck and we paid $50,000. Just think, you may be as lucky as she was."

Mike took out an accident/health/life insurance policy with a rider that in the event of an accidental fatality his beneficiary, Belle, would receive $1 million.

There was another time Ed encountered a ghost while taking a listing. This time, however, Mike brought the ghost home and planted him in the back yard. To Mike's and Belle's surprise the ghost suddenly grew into adulthood and eventually became a goaltender for the Edmonton Oil Kings hockey team.

Unfortunately in a game against the Medicine Tigers a MHT defenseman took a vicious slap shot and the ghost burst into flames.

To this day no one knows why the ghost burst into flames. Some suggested there could have been gun powder inside the puck and others that the entire Medicine Hat team was against monarchy.

Meanwhile a University of Alberta anthropologist began to do a study the incident and said that there was no magic bullet involved although he had heard of exploding fish but never of an exploding ghost. The anthropologist put the pieces together within a week and the ghost suddenly became the talk of the town lobbying Edmonton City Council for a Ghost monument commemorating the ghosts that died in Edmonton during the past century.

During his career Mike had to deal not only with ghosts but also with tramps. This occurred when a tramp stopped in front of the Best Realty office while Mike was sweeping the sidewalk and the tramp asked, "Any beer bottles or cans, sir?"

"Do I look like a man drinks so early in the morning?" Mike groaned.

"Pardon me, sir," the tramp continued. "I also collect vinegar bottles."

Another time a tramp approached Mike and said, "I'm blind. Can you spare $2.00 for a cup of coffee?" Mike was taken aback. "Isn't that a lot of money for a cup of coffee?"

"In Edmonton it ain't," the tramp said.

Ed handed the tramp a loony and in the process his handkerchief dropped to the ground. The tramp picked it up and returned it to Ed, which prompted Ed to say, "My good man. You aren't blind."

"I know, sir," the tramp said, "I'm working for my brother who is on a holiday in Hawaii."

Another time Mike handed a tramp a $5.00 bill and said, "I'm giving you this money not because you asked for it but it makes me feel good."

"If that is the case," the tramp said, "Why don't you give me a $10 bill and feel twice as good?"

The following day Mike's home brewed was so popular in the neighbourhood that he sent a sample to a laboratory to have it analyzed.

A week later the laboratory returned the sample with a note attached to the bottle, which in part read: "Dear Mr. Bike. Our conclusion is that your cow has diabetes."

Discouraged by the results of the analysis Mike used a keg of the home-brew to wet down the lawn, which encircled the cabin.

Watching this for several hours Belle could not restrain her curiosity any longer and said, "Ed, why are you using the beer on the lawn?"

"To keep the neighbourhood cats so they don't harm your budgie bird."

"But there are no cats within miles."

"See, it really works. Doesn't it?"

The same afternoon Belle caught Mike spraying his home-brew on the cow. According to Belle Ed sneaked up to the cow and sprayed the animal from head to tail.

When Belle asked, "Why are you spraying the cow with your home brew?" he replied, "I'm conducting Operation Cow Cow to make certain it isn't carrying hoof-and-mouth germs."

"But the cow hasn't got hoof-and-mouth disease," Belle insisted.

"Good," Mike said. "If it did it would spoil our milk supply, not to mention a shortage of cream for our porridge."

"And if the cow did have hoof-and-mouth disease, so what?"

"Just think of the number of bottles of Mike's Home Brew we'd sell to deodorize cows across Canada."

The following day Mike wrote a memo and posted it on a bulletin board at Very Best Realty. The memo read: As a Real Estate Salesman I have a Bad Day when:

- I wake up in the morning and Belle calls me Dominic instead of Mike.
- I arrive to list a house but the vendor has already listed with a competitor.
- I sell a home but the purchaser sues me because the measurements weren't accurate.
- Overnight, the mortgage rate increases 1% but now the prospect is unable to buy.
- On my way home from work my car's horn won't stop, and I'm following a gang of Hell's Angeles.
- I receive an offer to purchase and lose the deposit.
- I want to make a phone call but I'm out of quarters.
- The permanent crease in my trousers comes out.
- Sometimes my brain says *Go* but my body says *No.*
- When I think a saleslady's mini-skirt is a Freudian slip.

Listing real estate properties can be enjoyable but on one occasion it wasn't for Ed.

This happened when an enterprising housewife called all the real estate companies in Edmonton that she wanted a free market evaluation on her home and began house cleaning.

Next day her husband said in consternation "Hey, Peggy! There are 15 real estate salesmen from different companies to give a free appraisal of our home."

"Good," the wife replied. "Tell them to begin and when they hand you one, we will see their estimates and sell the home ourselves."

Puzzled by the rejection and the way the prospect behaved Mike went to see a fortune-teller for a possible explanation. While the fortune-teller was gazing into a crystal ball she did not have an answer but burst out with laughter.

"Why are you laughing?" Mike asked.

"Do you believe it? You are going to run for Mayor of Edmonton," the fortune-teller said and doubled up with laughter.

In a split second Mike smacked the fortune-teller's face.

"Why did you do that?" the fortune-teller said when she recovered.

Mike's answer was, "Because my agent, Very Best, always says to strike a happy medium."

CHAPTER 5

Mike Bike never behaved this way before. With 20 years experience as a realtor he did not demonstrate or attack establishment. "I'm kind of a realtor that doesn't cuss or fuss," Mike said to Belle showing displeasure.

"If I were you I would speak to Mayor Live about it. His worship has been mayor of Edmonton for over 10 years and should know something about handing out traffic tickets. I'm no lawyer but I think one could even argue it in court," Belle said.

What happened was that on an October afternoon Mike was showing property to a prospect, was caught in a radar speed trap and given a ticket for speeding. When Mike protested to the Chief of Police, who handed him the ticket, the Chief said, "Mike, we got you this time. We'll get the other realtors next time?" implying that all realtors were speeding demons.

Mike had received speeding tickets before so next morning along Jasper Avenue the Chief was a little mystified how carefully everyone was driving. Motorists were dead-on speed limit and smiled at the Chief as they passed his radar robot. Several blocks away Mike stood staging a one-man protest by holding a sign with bold letters that read; *Speed Trap Ahead*.

"Mike, you are distracting the attention of motorists," the Chief said, confiscated the sign and gave Mike a $100 ticket. Mike now had two tickets—one for speeding and the other for stunting.

"I guess I'll have to pay the two fines," Mike said to Belle.

Belle disagreed, "Not before you see the Mayor Live. Surely a citizen can stand beside a street holding up a sign. Is it not an attack on freedom of speech to criminalize an expression of opinion on a piece of board? If radar traps exist to slow down traffic in order to fund City Hall, fight it, there's a principle involved."

Mike took his wife's advice and when he confronted Mayor Live in his office where the atmosphere was electric as the Mayor Live said, "Mike, fight it in court if you wish but as long as I'm Mayor of Edmonton radar traps will continue on our streets. How else can the city pay for the upkeep of the Convention Centre, museum, the Arts Gallery, Olympic Stadium, hockey arenas and public swimming pools if not because of speed zones?"

"And if that's your position, I'll run for the Mayor's office myself," Mike said and went on, "I'm against speed traps for the sake of helping out with the City Hall treasury."

The Mayor burst out with laughter. When the laughter stopped continued, "Never, Never. If Edmonton elects you as mayor there will be a lot of disappointments."

Mike shot back, "You may be surprised."

When election time came in November the temperature was in the low teens, Celsius, and unseasonably cool and windy for Edmonton. A 60 km wind from the north rattled trees and scattered leaves on streets and sidewalks, a time Mike filed his nomination papers and to a group of supporters said, "I don't come bearing gifts. The only promise I make if elected mayor is that there will be no radar traps or a witch monument in our city."

Next day Mike held media press conference where he unveiled his platform and had hundreds of signs and pamphlets printed.

As the election date approached Mike had volunteers manning his headquarters that was a one-story building on Jasper Avenue that used to be a pizza parlour before the operator claimed bankruptcy.

The incumbent Mayor Live used a high-profile high-rise building on 101 Street that had lawyers, accountants, doctors and masseurs as tenants, as his headquarters.

Soon the campaign became one of the most hotly contested in Edmonton's history and turned into a case of personalities. The incumbent Live accused Mike of inexperience and Mike on the other hand accused the Mayor of driving tourists away from Edmonton because of the speed traps that he authorized.

Mike's campaign took him on streets and roads, which he had traveled on before. He knew each landmark and viewpoint always making his list of things that Calgary had and Edmonton needed. These, besides no radar traps, included a water fountain in front of City Hall, squirrels to feed in Hawrelak Park and at each entrance to the city a derrick mounted on a pedestal and a caption besides it with the words *WELCME TO THE OIL CAPITAL OF CANADA.*

Mike's strength was that part north of the river where a mix of diverse cultures lived. In this part of the city Mike found Ukrainians of heritage who wanted compensation for being wrongly incarcerated as 'Austrians' during the First World War. The Japanese wanted compensation for being wrongly incarcerated during the World War11.

Those of Chinese heritage wanted recognition for being mistreated during the time the Canadian Pacific Railway was built through the Rocky Mountains in the 1880's and being stereotyped as laundry and café operators, herbalists and acupuncturists. The Irish wanted a plaque at the Library dedicated to George Bernard Shaw. Shaw apparently after visiting Edmonton began growing a beard. The Italians wanted Caboto Park renovated so they could hold a larger picnic on Columbus Day. Francophone's wanted separate schools from English one's and First Nation people wanted their land claims settled.

Belle suggested that a monument be built to the witches who were hanged in 1892 but Mike refused to include the request as part of his platform even after Belle said to him over a cup of tea, "I'm a descendent of one of the witches."

The following week Mike spoke to the Chamber of Commerce and said to the members that he was in favour banks staying open on Sundays. He walked along major Edmonton streets and talked and shook hands with merchants there.

At a meeting of the Bird Watchers Society Mike said that he would not harm the Canada geese that leave doo doo on beaches, golf courses and sidewalks but would find an electronic automated contraption that would frighten the birds away.

Next Mike stopped at the Union Office and said to its members, "I'm in favour of increasing the minimum wage and getting people off welfare." At a right moment he said, "Why doesn't the union open a Food Bank?"

Mike also stopped at a High School and queried the principal about students spending their lunch period at video arcades and in many cases, "Coming home with illicit drugs?"

At the Royal Alex Hospital Mike asked the administrator why the Emergency Unit wasn't completed. When the administrator said it was the Provincial Government's fault Mike said, "Then take down the sign saying *Construction Will Start Soon*. The sign has been up five years already."

That evening after Mike and Belle enjoyed the epic movie *The Miracle* they were having supper at the *Red Lobster* restaurant and since Mike was well known, people stopped at their table. Each time Mike would tell them about the giant fish he caught in the North Saskatchewan River. After a while Belle whispered, "Honey, I think it's nice that so many people speak to you and I see nothing wrong with you telling them about the fish but each time you speak to them the size of the fish is increased. Why in the world do you do that?"

"I know these people. They are voters and I want them to trust me at my word. So I make it a practice never to tell them more than I think they believe," Mike said.

Mike, through his experience as a real estate salesman displayed an uncanny knack of connecting with concerns of common people and mixed with them in bars, in restaurants and on streets. In order to garner votes Mike played pool with the firemen at the Fire Hall, took part in a golf tournament, attended a baseball game where a foul ball hit him on the head thus energizing his brain. Mike also attended a demolition derby where a driver thought Mike wouldn't win the election to which Mike replied, "No one ever went broke estimating the intelligence of Edmonton voters. I believe my chances of winning are good."

The chances definitely improved the following day when Mayor Live and Mike attended a luncheon sponsored by the Edmonton Real Estate Board and the Mayor said, "If Edmonton gets rid of radar traps then the residents will have to pay more taxes."

The following day Mike spoke with City Hall employees where a file clerk said, "Sir, how about the Edmonton Beauty Pageant?"

"How about it?" Mike said to the clerk who looked like an overweigh parrot in Hawaiian jeans.

"Do you like bathing beauties?"

"I can't tell because I never bathed one but I'll tell you Edmonton women are the most beautiful in the world."

No matter where Mike went he was all eyes and ears taking notes of voter desires and their complaints. Many of those who retired in Edmonton and came from the Prairie provinces, said they would vote for Mike Bike not because when he visited Regina a television news clip showed a dog mistaking him for a fire hydrant but because when Ed purchased rental properties in the city he did not jack up the rent immediately and of Mike's profile.

Mike's visit with a retired couple from Prince Albert, Saskatchewan was particularly interesting, not that Prime Minister Diefenbaker practiced law there but because the wife had just made a saskatoon pie which Mike enjoyed and she gave him the recipe.

As Mike increased his hectic pace he visited the Royal Canadian Legion where he said to a group of veterans over a glass of beer, "You should have better pensions."

Ed also went to solicit votes from Reverend Taylor, Father McCarthy, Rabbi Libowitch and farmer Jerry Fix who at the time had some corn beside him so Mike said, "Jerry, what are you doing?"

"I'm doing what I'd like to do with incumbent mayor. I'm pulling its ears.

It did occur to me that Live spelled backwards is Evil. Mayor Live is a grumpy old lawyer that I cannot trust. Unseating him as Mayor of Edmonton is a must."

In days that followed Mike picked up votes after participating in three-legged, sack-jumping and spoon-egg carrying contests at the Edmonton October Rodeo and Fall Fair where Belle had entered her rooster, Mario, at the Rooster Crowing Contest where twelve rooster finalists, ranging from tiny bantams to hulking Rhode Island Reds, were kept in boxes until the last possible moment and then placed in separate cages on a table. The rooster with the most crows in ten minutes won. Spectators were encouraged to egg the roosters on with their own attempts to cock-a-doodle-doo a song.

Well, Mario, who survived many of his chicken friends being slaughtered, could make hens weep by simply opening his beak, filled a chicken coup full of people with his plaintive song by crowing 8 impressive times within a space of 10 minutes. His nearest competitor crowed seven.

Mario's were sharp cock-a-doodle-doos, sensitive and evocative. When Mario, who had 5 distinctive spikes on his comb and a pearly white plumage, crowed, he raised his wings, stretched out his neck and a cock-a-doodle-doo emerged.

While Mario was pouring out his talent, heads turned, voices lowered, infants stopped crying in their mother's arms and even Mario's opponents, some who were three times his size, appeared to be awed.

And in a contest where most cock-a-doodle-doo's within the allotted time wins, that made the other roosters also rans and Belle's entry eventual winner.

In the evening as the Rodeo and Fall Fair continued Expo Complex was filled with people and while a band played Mike and Belle spun around dancing until past midnight. By now many Edmontonions felt Mike Bike had become not only a fine dancer but also an extraordinary candidate for the office of Mayor.

In the final week of his campaign Mike knocked on doors for the second time striking up conversations with homemakers, and if there were babies inside, he made every effort to kiss them too. Wherever there were two people, Mike was the third.

Mike's advertisements in Edmonton newspapers began to appear larger and larger and more frequent. He also doubled his distribution of leaflets, billboards, lawn signs and car bumper stickers.

During this time Mayor Live was busy too. His newspaper ads appeared much larger and like Mike, advertised on the radio and television. That was the week Belle came to Ed's campaign headquarters to monitor the switchboard and answer calls from the public.

"You should find it easy," Mike said, "When answering the phone just say 'Mike Bike campaign headquarters' and if you aren't sure about an enquiry tell the caller I'll call back."

"I'll do my best," Belle said as Mike stepped out the door to do more electioneering.

The first caller that Belle had to deal with was a woman who wanted to know where to vote. When Belle told her, there was a dial tone. After the phone ran again Belle answered, "Good afternoon. Mike Bike campaign headquarters."

"Is this the campaign manager?" a male voice asked.

"No, but maybe I can help you."

"Okay. Tell Mr. Bike I wouldn't vote for him even if he was the only candidate alive."

"Why is that?"

"Because I hate politicians and furthermore, when he had my home listed for sale, he never did sell it."

The phone cliqued again and Belle began licking envelopes. When the phone rang the next time she let it ring four times before she answered.

"God afternoon, dear." a female voice said at the other end. "My name is Elsie Brunet. Will you please tell Mr. Bike that I will need a ride on Election Day?"

"Are you going to vote for Mike?'

"No, but I might as well save on gas for the incumbent mayor."

It was several minutes later that the phone rang again. The caller identified herself as a cat lover and asked if Mike won the election would city council introduce a cat bylaw. Belle did not know the answer so she told the caller that Ed would call her personally.

The same caller then asked, "Is Mr. Bike in favour of building a witch monument in the city?"

"Definitely not but I'm in favour."

"You are in favour of a witch monument. Why?"

"Because I'm a descendent of one of the three witches who were hanged in the city in 1892."

"If that is the case I'll tell my friends and neighbours not to vote for him."

There was another clique and the phone line was dead. Following several more phone calls Belle began to regret that she had volunteered to monitor the switchboard for Ed. When another volunteer came to replace her Belle said, "Everything was all right with the exception that I might have lost Mr. Bike votes."

"Why is that?" the replacement asked.

"Because some of the callers were rude so I told them to go and jump into the North Saskatchewan River."

In the final week of the campaign Mike and Mayor Live appeared at a public forum, which was televised on a community cable channel. Mike debated that he was against speeding radar traps because on the account of them, tourist did not stop in Edmonton but continued traveling either to Calgary or Grande Prairie.

Mayor Live meanwhile stuck to the theory that speed traps were the best way to upkeep public buildings and that Mike was too young to understand municipal politics and above all his lack of experience. "From the income derived we are able to maintain public buildings without going to a bank and paying high interest on a loan."

The following day Mike purchased 60 minutes of airtime on radio station CHED and took calls from listeners. At the beginning the callers asked serious questions about taxes, parking meters, snow clearing, potholes on streets and a possible cat bylaw. As the program progressed, however, hecklers turned the program into a *Comedy Hour*.

"Hey, Mr, Bike," a listener phoned. "Do you have enough money for a rainy day should you lose the election?'

In reply Mike said, "I never shop on a rainy day."

The same listener then said that he saw Mike campaigning at the Doodle Strudel Noodle Restaurant and asked, "How did you find the meal?"

Mike's response was, "With a magnifying glass."

Another caller complained, "As a mayoralty candidate you don't seem to know which side of your bread is buttered," to which Mike replied, "What does it matter? I eat both sides."

When Mike looked towards the clock he discovered that he had little airtime left so he said to his audience, "Remember, folks, tomorrow get out and vote. The polls open at 8:00 in the morning and close at 8:00 in the evening."

On a November, 16th 1975 Election Day Mike and Belle voted as soon as the polls opened and Mike's and Belle's parents came to campaign headquarters to help voters who needed a ride to the polling station.

After casting their ballot Mike went to campaign headquarters contemplating victory and triumph, and Belle to the Fairmont McDonald Hotel to assist in preparing a possible victory party.

As soon as the polls closed Mike went to City Hall to watch counting of the ballots by the returning officer. Minutes later Mayor Live appeared too. As the ballots were counted Mayor Live took the lead, only a short time later to be passed by Mike. There were more lead changes in position than Elizabeth Taylor had husbands. In the end Mike Bike won the election with a plurality of 1,179 votes and his victory speech ended with, "Everyone who know me knows that I'm a fighter. Let me say one more thing. I want to thank my wife, Belle, for standing and sitting behind me during the election campaign."

Outgoing Mayor Live took he defeat with dignity and after congratulating Mike on the upset victory said, "I don't know what happened. I assume there will be no more radar traps from this day onward?"

"Absolutely," Mike said. "As soon as I'm installed into the mayor's office I'll have the speed traps discontinued."

The defeated Mayor Live then said, "Mike, you never did mention in your campaign how City Council is going to pay for the upkeep of the public buildings."

"Simple," Mike said, "Edmonton will be host to the largest Fishing Derby Alberta has ever seen and the proceeds will be more than necessary for their upkeep."

"Correct me, if I'm wrong but you must have meant to say the city will host the world curling bonspiel?"

'I'll do nothing of the sort. I did say a *Fishing Derby* which, with council's approval, will be held during the first week in August. And do you want to know something else?"

"You riding on a broom won't be a pretty sight, especially during Halloween?"

"No, this isn't a joking matter," Mike said, "The fisherman who catches the largest fish and there are many species, including walleye, pike, whitefish and trout, will win $1-million as first prize."

"And the second?"

"A one year supply of fish and chips donated by Joey's Fish and Chips Restaurant."

"Give me a break," Live said, "One-million dollars? Edmonton can hardly afford such a generous prize."

"But it can."

"How?"

"Through corporate sponsoring."

On the day Mayor-elect Mike Bike took office he was euphoric because city council unanimously agreed not to hold an international fishing derby of this magnitude at some far away lake but the North Saskatchewan River which crosses Edmonton and flows between the towns of Devon and Fort Saskatchewan.

News of the Derby first appeared on the front page of the J*ournal* accompanied by a photograph of the city of Edmonton. The major wire services picked up the story and flashed it to correspondents around the world making it global in scope, including the CBC, BBC, CNN and Fox News, Washington Post and Moscow's Time.

Initially the idea of a Fish Derby was almost on the verge of collapsing as there were all sorts of glitches, the event was absolutely mind-blowing which made Mayor Bike nervous but then thanks to the compassionate help of hundreds of volunteers and participants things got better and those living in and around Edmonton got excited as the community was literally transformed by a pre-derby construction boom.

Highways to Fort Saskatchewan, Devon and Saint Albert were resurfaced, bridges within the city given a new coat of paint and even the observation tower at the Municipal Airport was renovated. The fishing boundary was set between Devon and Fort Saskatchewan

For those not familiar with the city of Edmonton and to stimulate interest in the Derby the Chamber of Commerce issued a brochure implying that the city was power house and a hot bed for entrepreneurs and that if foreign fishermen weren't' familiar with Edmonton:

One must first learn to pronounce the name. It's, Ed-mon-ton and not Ed-mon-chuk.

The Chamber of Commerce also printed a road map showing directions and that Edmonton was a city of nearly a million people, the capital of the province Alberta, the oil capital of Canada and the beef capital of Alberta based by the number of hamburgers McDonald's sold each month.

The minimum acceptable speed on Jasper Avenue is 60 miles an hour. Anything above is considered downright outrageous.

Car horns are actually 'Road Rage" indicators.

If while driving someone has actually their turn signal on, it's probably a factory defect.

Streets mysteriously change their names as soon as you cross the intersection.

All ladies with blue hair driving a Cadillac have the right of way. Period.

In asking directions you must know how to speak Ukrainian or French.

During an Oiler or Eskimo game if some guy with a flag tries to get you to park in his yard you should run over him. It's probably not his yard anyway.

During an upgrade three lane streets suddenly change to 2 lanes and vice versa, two lanes turn to three.

Forget the traffic rules you learned elsewhere. Edmonton has its own version—Hold on and Pray.

If you suddenly stop at a yellow light, you will be rear ended.

The morning rush hour is from 6 to 11. The evening rush hour is from 1 to 7. Friday rush hours are 6 a.m. until midnight.

For safety sake during night time it's advisable to travel in pairs and ignore aggressive pan-handlers.

Prior to the Fishing Derby opening s survey was conducted by SuveyMonkey as to which was a better sport—Having Sex or Fishing? 90 percent answered that Fishing indeed was better and gave reason why:

The Ten Commandments don't say anything against Fishing

No matter how much you had to drink you still can Fish

It's perfectly acceptable to pay a professional to Fish with you

You don't have to go to a sleezy shop in a sleezy neighbourhood to buy Fishing stuff

Your Fishing partner will never say, "Not again? We just fished last week. Is fishing all you think about?"

Nobody expects you to Fish with the same partner for the rest of your life

Nobody will ever tell you that you may go blind if you go fishing

When you are dealing with Fishing pro, you never have to wonder if they are really an undercover cop

Nobody expects you to give up Fishing if your partner loses interest in you

Following the survey a state of the art wharf was built connecting the river front with an easy access to Churchill Square the fish weigh-in site, along with an information booth where one can avoid traffic circles, twists and turns and find an alternate route to find things to do, eat, sleep and relieve themselves just in case . . . .

The first sign to appear at the Square was: *Coca Cola Welcomes All Fishermen*. And the Coke cans were white in color with a photo of North Saskatchewan River fish imprinted on them.

At the municipal curling rinks volunteers would serve breakfast, and more signs throughout the city read: *Molson's* the official beer, *Royal Bank* the official bank and *Sun Life* the official insurer. There were other official sponsors too and it seemed each corporation listed in the top 500 in *Fortune Magazine* were sponsoring one thing or another.

This included *Raid* the official mosquito repellent sponsor and *Toledo* the official scale to weigh the fish on. *Duracell* agreed to be the official battery and *Visa* the official credit card. Each sponsor agreed to pay $100,000 to have its name and logo displayed in around Edmonton for the duration of the derby. This included their logo imprinted in the ice and sideboards in the arena and curling rinks.

The creative financing did not end there. Mayor Bike concocted a deal with the private sector where City Council sold public building names and services to private companies for a substantial fee during the Derby. For $50,000 one could have city buses wrapped with advertisements. If $50,000 was too rich one could have a company logo placed on the garbage truck driving up and down back alleys.

Lawyers could advertise on police cars for $50 a day and for several dollars more they could ride in the cruiser and sign up clients as soon as they were handcuffed and interviewed. And then there was City Hall itself. *Esso* jumped at the opportunity to have its name linked with the building implying the oil company owned it. *Burger King* sponsored the Tourist office. *Asprin* the hospitals, *Dairy Queen* the library.

The Convention *Centre to* Shaw Convention Centre and *Ford* the museum. Olympic Stadium was changed to Rexall Place the local baseball stadium to Telus Field and the Edmonton Science Centre to the Telus Science Centre.

Goodyear Tire agreed to send its blimp for aerial shots of the Derby. Council also approved user fees for the municipal airport public washrooms.

Cash-strapped Edmonton Public School Board agreed to initiate rooftop advertising. The huge ads appeared visible only from flying aircraft and students on ground level didn't see them.

The revenue derived from this form of advertising was allocated to purchase badly needed equipment, supplies and increase teacher salaries.

The streets were decorated with murals of variety of heads of fish, birds and animals in the area.

At the same time Mural-a-mania spread like wild fire even to garbage cans as local artists lent their talent to decorate Edmonton for the time Mayor Bike would stand on a podium, wave his magic wand and say, "Awesome! Let the Fishing Derby begin!"

There were also garbage can murals with pictures of celebrities who had previously visited Edmonton and included author Bernard Shaw and the Prince of Wales. A different private company sponsored each can but if one sponsored 100 cans it was entitled to a 10% discount.

Of course the Derby sponsorship wasn't just a wealthy corporation paying out a sum of money to be a sponsor so that it wouldn't have to pay federal taxes. It was people who paid $5.00 each in order to personally meet with a participating fisherman and see who could tell the silliest fishing story. For an extra dollar a contestant autographed his/her fishing license with proceeds going to the Edmonton 'Stop Bullying' Foundation.

As the date for the Derby drew nearer there was a parade through Edmonton, a Miss Derby Pageant, a fashion show displaying the latest fishing wear, a Spelling Bee of fish names and paraphernalia associated with the fishing industry, an all-star cast of retired World fishermen pitted against those in North America in a fly casting contest. The flies were couriered from Yellowknife, North West Territories for the occasion.

Finding accommodation in Edmonton suddenly became difficult as all hotels; motels, lodges campgrounds, High School and College dorms and church basements were reserved in advance. There was so much interest in the Derby that even a cruise ship operator in Florida wanted to know if a ship could dock in Edmonton.

Finding a hotel room became difficult. Daily rates skyrocketed by 50% and the price of a glass of beer by fifty cents. At the Armada Hotel for example, the general manager said, "Extra beds and cots have been placed in rooms. We have been sold out since an ad appeared in *Field and Stream* magazine. Derby fever has indeed taken Edmonton by storm. This is something huge and popular forcing us to add more hotel rooms."

The manager of the Coast Hotel said something similar and continued, "We had requests for blocks of space since Christmas."

At our hotel not only have we fishermen booked from France, United States but also England which shares its British colonial heritage with Canada and a thirst for strong beer."

One entrepreneur advertised that he was willing to rent his home for $1000 a day. As it turned out the home was in Calgary but that did not matter because Sheik Mohammad Abdul from Saudi Arabia, rented it and in his private jet flew to Calgary back and forth until the Derby was over.

There were hundreds of entry forms printed and paid for as soon as the Derby was advertised in foreign countries. Most of the contestants who entered were heads of state, sports, TV and Hollywood celebrities. There could have been some criminals too but no one could tell by the fishing gear they used.

In Edmonton the city gets blizzards in the winter and hurricanes in the summer. Tornadoes, ice storms and thunder storms are all part of the environment equation but fortunately the local forecast was for mild sunny weather with no rain or high winds in sight, ideal conditions to catch the 'big one' during the Derby

Local residents who did not enter could experience the fish weigh-ins by watching coverage on CBC television that had rights to televise the occasion. CBC in turn sold rights to every major network including Albania and Zimbabwe.

On August 5 sport fishermen from throughout the world, after paying a handsome entry fee, congregated in Edmonton thus giving the city and the sponsors a lot of publicity.

On the first day of the Derby men with fishing rods and landing nets, along with tourists and visitors with bottles of whisky hidden in their backpacks poured into the city.

Besides catching tonnes of fish and hundreds of volunteers making the derby a success here are several amusing incidents fishermen experienced.

The first incident, which was extensively described by a CBC announcer, took place when a Hollywood starlet got into a fight with a pesky pelican.

The actress had landed a fish but the pelican had his eyes open on the fish too and followed it right onto the boat where the bird nabbed the hook, line and sinker.

The actress, who had just won an Academy Award, wasn't going to give up her prize without a struggle.

As the bird took of with the fish and yards and yards of line, she hung on to the rod and succeeded in realing the fish in until the thief was within grabbing distance.

But as the actress was struggling to pluck the fish from the pelican's bill she dropped the fish into the water below. The pelican quickly dove down to take hold of what he considered was his dinner. Easier said than done the pelican missed his target. Since the fish was still on the line the actress hauled it in as fast as she could, popped it into a basket and snapped on the lid.

The pelican, infuriated and having been done out of his meal came up from behind and gave the actress a spiteful peck on her posterior causing her to fall into the water knocking over the basket. As the lid flowed away, the pelican went into action.

He seized the actress's fish, and taking no chances this time, swallowed it down then and there.

Another amusing incident took place when Pastor Taylor tried his luck at catching the largest fish but tragedy struck when the weather forecast was wrong and a sudden storm blew over and destroyed his boat.

Pastor Taylor barely escaped with his life. Being a religious man the priest picked up his *Bible* and read:

"The Lord gives and the Lord takes and I shall bear the cause."

When the storm was over the Reverend set out fishing again but before he reached the shore of the river a bear attacked him and in the process broke the pastor's arm. From the *Bible* Father Taylor read, "The Lord gives and the Lord takes and I shall bear the cause."

Pastor Taylor oh, did he ever love to fish. He was a determined fisherman and wasn't about to withdraw from the Derby so with his good hand he picked up a hook, line and sinker and was on his way fly-casting.

With the first toss of the hook, the pastor caught his rear-end leaving the devout man in terrible pain.

Looking up above Pastor Taylor said, "Lord, what did I do ever wrong to deserve this?"

A *Superior* voice answered, "Pastor Taylor, there something about you that browns me off."

"And what may that be?"

"Instead of participating in the Edmonton Fishing Derby you should be paying more attention to your parishioners and convince them to put paper bills instead of coins into the collection basket."

A fisherman from the Philippines launched his boat at 4 a. m. and after making himself comfortable accidentally dropped his chewing gum into the water.

The moment the gum hit the surface a gigantic pike snapped it. A moment later he dropped the gum again and a walleye snapped it too.

As an experienced fisherman in Manila Jun de la Cruz continued to drop his gum into the river and as the fish came up he batted each over the head with his oar and hauled them out one after another.

Near the end of the Derby there was curiosity among fisherman as to why a fisherman from Malaysia was catching only large fish. "This Derby is fixed!" a fisherman from Poland protested and demanded that the Derby inspector, who was from France, find out what the fisherman was using for bait.

When the inspector began his investigation he initially used binoculars and spotting scopes but then when he dove into the bottom of the river found a perogi.

As the inspector surfaced he concluded that why the Pole was catching so many large fish was because he used a perogi as bait. The inspector concluded, "Upon close scrutiny I found Mr. Polanski attaches a perogi to his hook, drops the hook into the river and as the perogi unfurls, the fish get excited and voila, latch on to the hook."

As soon as the inspector said those words a fisherman from Norway let out a scream that could be heard halfway across the county of Strathcona, "Hey! I caught something huge and it's not a bass, pike or a white fish but one that his huge, really huge. Please someone help me to pull it to shore!"

Initially those watching thought the Norwegian hooked on to the monster Ogopogo which had moved from the Okanagan Lake in British Columbia to the North Saskatchewan River because Alberta had no provincial taxes. If that was true can you imagine how many British Columbians would be moving to Alberta?

It turned out to be a 9 foot, 800 pound, 100 year old sturgeon.

Those watching the Norwegian and other fishermen tug and pull were at awe as his wife ran down the dock with a large net and Mayor Bike with a camera. Following the sturgeon being weighed Edmonton was overrun with reporters as Mayor Mike Bike declared, "Congratulations Sven Jenson you have latched on to the largest fish and have won first prize. I now declare the first Edmonton Fishing Derby officially over!"

And all the volunteers who sold the most T-shirts were taken out to Pizza Hut and treated to a gigantic thank you pizza. For the remaining volunteers they had to share a large, really large cake with a lot of icing on top courtesy the Italian Bakery.

To the postal workers in Edmonton Mayor Bike said. "I'm sorry, and to everyone who ordered a T-shirt, I say thank you for your boundless patience. If you got a T-shirt that vaguely resembled your original order, you did much, much better than most fishermen."

As soon as the Derby was over SurveyMonkey conducted three surveys among the foreign fishermen: (1) What they didn't like about Edmonton. (2) What they did like about Edmonton and (3) Why the foreign fishermen were often late in trying to catch the largest fish.

What foreign Fishermen Did Not Like About Edmonton

1. Too many stop lights and traffic circles
2. Too many aggressive panhandlers
3. Not enough public lavatories
4. Too many pigeon drops on sidewalks
5. Too many hotels with bed bugs.
6. Too many stabbings, home invasions and homicides
7. Too many mosquitoes
8. Weeds not attended at commercial parking lots
9. Has unreliable weather forecasters
10. Too many private liquor stores which leads to drunkenness

What Foreign Fishermen Liked About Edmonton

1. Hookers that were available on 118 Avenue
2. The number of liquor stores available to purchase whisky and beer
3. The number of shopping malls where foreign fishermen can purchase 'I Have been to Edmonton' T-shirts
4. Edmonton residents were kind, considerate and patient while giving directions
5. Visit nearby Elk Island Park and in conducting a self-guided tour view roaming herds of elk, bison and moose and 250 species of birds
6. While not fishing, a fisherman can go to one of 70 different golf course where
   During mid-summer golf days are 17 hours long
7. Visit Fort Edmonton Park, Canada's living history museum
8. Can do bungee jumping from the High Level bridge
9. Enjoy a pizza at Peters Pizza in Spruce Grove
10. Edmonton has some of the prettiest women in the world

Why Foreign Fishermen were often late during the Derby

1. Long line-ups at McDonald's and Wendy's
2. Moose and deer crossing the streets
3. Temporarily lost keys to the car and boat
4. Unexpected family emergency back home
5. Attending a blow-out sale is more important than being 10 minutes late
6. Missed an oncoming bus

7. Argued with other fishermen before going to fish
8. Roosters failed to crow in the morning
9. Had a migraine headache
10. Staying up late enjoying a glass of whisky or beer

CHAPTER 6

In 1981 Canadians were embarrassed when the Soviet Union defeated Canada and won the *Canada Cup* in the World International hockey tournament. Wayne Gretzky along with thousands wept because of the loss. So did Mike weep but shortly after recovered and was excited too because he was able to celebrate his 50th birthday and after one term as mayor of Edmonton acquired full ownership of the Very Best Realty agency and changed the name to Bike Realty Ltd. The deal was complicated and completed only after Ed offered a 10% commission discount to any vendor should their property be sold. This of course annoyed some of his competitors and even Belle said he shouldn't have done it. Negotiating the complex sale contract between Very Best Realty and Ed Bike was difficult which at the end Mike's response was: "If you own the company you have to climb the corporate ladder. In my opinion it's the best deal any one has made since the Boston Red Sox sold Babe Ruth to the New York Yankees in 1919. At any rate Bike Realty Ltd, has to expand its operation and move to a new location."

After the dust was cleared Mike sat down with Belle and discussed the proposed new office and made a list of things that were critical in the future success of the company.

These items included:

Additional staff
A cellular phone and a measuring tape for each individual salesman
A pair of grey pants and a blue blazer with the Bike Realty crest on it.
A talking alarm clock so that the salesman wakes up on time.
A pair of winter boots just in case there's a winter snow storm.
A shiatsu pup so when the salesman is out of town the wife has someone to talk too
Digital camera
And a snowmobile

As far as the office, it was situated on the first floor of the City Centre Mall where the parking wasn't as adequate as before and the rent a bit higher. But to Mike that did not matter, what did was that because of the tar sands oil boom near Fort McMurray and Cold Lake there was heavier traffic at the mall with perspective buyers wishing to buy and vendor wishing to sell.

City Centre Mall of course is situated in the centre of the city near City Hall where one could find the latest local real estate statistics, Winspear Centre where one could listen to An Edmonton Symphony concert, Alberta Arts Centre, where one could view a Monet and a Picasso.

The Stanley Milner Public Library was easily accusable and one could read anything one wanted to know about the real estate industry.

And L'Exspresso Café that served the best gourmet, organic coffee and donuts without necessarily have to have a prescription. All buildings were surrounded by the Sir Winston Churchill Square which earlier was the North Saskatchewan River Fish Derby weigh-in location.

The office was huge with wooden floors lacquered in shining white and a modern kitchen with a coffee maker, to enjou coffee during a break, a microwave oven to warm up potato chips and a large refrigerator to keep beer in and a stylish stone bathroom. A 24 foot oval white marble conference table was the centre piece of the conference room designed to impress clients, and a 24 hour alarm system.

So the new office was opened. Now Mike needed someone to help and run it. Belle who by now became computer literate advertised on Job Bank, Kijiji and Craigslist and within a week received more than 50 applications. Mike interviewed a bunch of great candidates but none as great as Chritisan Paliganas his own house keeper. Christian was enthusiastic, tireless, had a sense of humour and previous experience as a clerk in the Philippines with the Lucio Tan conglomerate in processing Chowking and Jollibee restaurants. This for Mike was a blessing.

Christian had since become a Canadian citizen and accepted full time employment with company benefits which included a lucrative pension plan, free health and dental care and the ability to spend a three week holiday visiting her family during Christmas in Southern Leyte. With Christian on board it made everything feel different. Not better or worse. Just a lot more serious.

A day after Christian was employed Mike got serious but at the same time surprised when he opened his computer and on Face Book noticed that Christian had already posted an invitation to his 50th birthday party that read:

On November 8 Uncle Mike Bike will be 50 years old and if you are planning to attend his birthday party please do not bring gifts of underwear, neckties and T-shirts. Since the theme of the party is Filipino you are encouraged to bring odobo, bagoong. lechon and pancit. If you can't bring the above bring $50 in cash which will be given to a Philippine charity or 2000 pesos instead. And please no rice as there is a rice shortage in the Philippines.

Christian received 100 responses that they would attend but Jessa Benito who was employed by Century 21, a rival company, that she couldn't bring the above but Recipe # 5 soup and balut would be available and asked if Canada Tire money could be a substitute.

Christian commented:

> Dear Jessa
>
> Don't be funny, the suggested soup and balut are aphrodisiacs and uncle Bike has no need of the above at this time. And Canada tire money isn't a legal tender. Here's what you do if you really want to attend the party. Contact my former Philippine employer Lucio Tan and he might be interested in helping you.

Tell Mr. T the pesos will go to a charity so that poverty stricken children in Tomas Oppus, Southern Leyte can go to school.

Jessa commented:

I contacted Lucio Tan and also the richest man in the Philippines, Henry Sy, and both billionaires declined to help me. Mr. Tan said he's unable to help because he's opening more Jollibee and Chowking restaurants by expanding in Asia and Dubai in the United Arab Emirates. And Henry Sy said that his 41 shopping malls and hotels are undergoing a massive renovation program and his bank has fewer customers than the year before.

Christian commented:

Problem, problem, the rich make money and the poor make babies. Here's what you do. Contact President Gloria Arroyo and see what she says about you attending the birthday party.

Jessa commented:

I couldn't get in touch with President Arroyo because she's preparing for the upcoming election but her secretary said no donation would be forthcoming because of the recent Muslim insurgency in Mindanao, an earthquake in Manila, a monsoon in Samar, a flood in Laguna and a landslide in Saint Bernard. The recovery cost is prohibitive. But I want to tell you something, "At age 50 Uncle Mike probably needs a walking cane, a walker and Viagra."

Christian commented:

Jessa, you really need a holiday. I'm told that Uncle Mike tried Viagra when he was in his late forties but Belle his wife, got angry and threw the pills into a neighbour's yard \where the chickens ate the pills one after another. And do you want something—the chickens are now laying hard boiled eggs.

So let's go to the top and contact Pope Benedict 11 in the Vatican. 80% of Filipino's are Catholic so he may consider your request. But please don't contact the Queen of England because she may want to buy the Philippines and take over ruling the 7,101 islands like the Americas did in 1898.

Jessa commented:

I've been chatting so much that I feel I need a holiday. But there's good news.

Benedict 11 is busy dealing with the church sex scandals but his secretary suggested that I attend mass at the Basilica in Edmonton and a special collection will be taken to help solve my problem

Christian commented:

Awesome! Good news. I always believed a prayer could solve problems. Keep me posted.

Jessa Commented:

> I attended the Sunday mass at the Basilica on Jasper Avenue and a special collection took place which is great. I'm keeping $80.00 so that I can attend Uncle. Bike's birthday party and the balance I have sent to the Philippines so the kids in Tomas Oppus can go to school and get an education which I never had. And you know something? Twelve kids had no shoes and a day later each wanted a laptop and a cell phone.

On November 7th there was a snow storm in Edmonton and the worst was still to come when on the 8th the temperature dropped to—30C and flights to the International Airport were cancelled or rerouted. Christian kept her breath as she said to anyone who cared to listen. "A fiesta is part of Filipino culture. Through bad weather and even bad times Uncle Mike's birthday must go on."

In the ballroom of the Fairmont Hotel MacDonald those that acknowledge kept coming to the big bash. Among the guests were the Filipino consular general from Vancouver and the Mayor of Edmonton and their wives and adding to the excitement was the presence of Belle to sing country and western songs and gorgeous Jessa Benito doing magical card tricks.

Soon there were the rhythmic pounding of the drums and before anyone knew it shuffling of feet, shaking heads, waving hands—and joining revellers in their Sunday best clothing in a merriment mood. Amid this confusion those wishing Mike a "Happy Birthday" drank Mike's home brewed beer.

The fiesta-like occasion featured a tapestry of Filipino food, karaoke singing and dancing. For putting the party together Christian was given 'Thank You' applause from everyone. Raffles, promotions and giveaways were a persistent counterpoint as the crowd swelled, eager for the night's performance and to meet Mike in person.

As the evening entertainment drew near, scattered buzzes of excitement began to arise, from mouths lathed in sweets and content from samples of authentic Filipino food (buffet style) that included baloong, odobo, lechon and pancit and of course plenty of noodles and rice.

Once the evening was in full swing there were cheers, shouting and hand clapping and a sense of coming as Ed's birthday cake was brought out with 50 candles which Mike had difficulty in blowing out.

At the close individual's shook Mike's hand wishing him another 50 years of good health, happiness and wealth. With the food that was left over, Christian donated it to the Edmonton Food Bank.

By now Mike's new office was stuffed with: "Happy Birthday" and "Thank You" cards and monthly performance results with his name always near the top. Numerous framed awards: Salesman Of the Year, The Multi-Million Dollar Sales Club, the Vwery Best Realty President Club along with lifetime achievement awards lined the walls. Since Mike married Belle and hired Christian, Bike Realty Ltd. had done exceptionally well.

"Serving people not selling real estate," is how Mike viewed his job and he loved doing it. "I can't visualize not getting up in the morning and people not needing me," Mike said to Belle when she asked him about the possibility of an early retirement

Mike declined suggestion even after Belle said, "We can find a place where we can look out a window, past our gardener, who is busily pruning mango, papaya and jack fruit trees, sparkling with sunlight. The sky is clear blue. The sea is a deeper blue, sparking with sunlight. A gentle breeze comes drifting in from the ocean, clean and refreshing, as our maid brings us breakfast while we are in bed."

Are you talking about Victoria, British Columbia?' Mike asked.

"No but this paradise isn't in Mecca, Dubai the Caribbean or the Mediterranean but Boracay island in the Philippines voted second out of 25 finest beaches in the world and living on the island is affordable, in fact, it costs only one-half as much as living in Edmonton."

Ed said that retirement was interesting but his dream had not yet been fulfilled as he wanted to try his hand in federal politics.

One of the first things Ed did as the sole proprietor of Very Best Realty was to write an exam that made him a full-time agent. The following day he met with his co—salesmen and said to them, "Since becoming owner and agent of Very Best Realty I have noticed that some of the salesmen are using mumbo-jumbo language in the exchange of normal verbal communication with relation to the performance of routine sales activities."

From his jacket pocket Mike pulled out a sheet of paper that contained code numbers and then pinned the sheet on the bulletin board and proceeded, "This code is provided to permit individual freedom and originality of our fellow salesmen to alleviate frustration and provide a leaner, precise and effective means of communication with one another. And not to offend client relationship and other individuals with sensitive ears that may be within hearing distance.

To preclude mistaking the communication codes with the department numbers and telephone extensions, management has assigned 800 and 900 series of numbers to be utilized for convenience and clarity."

The code numbers and what they meant are as follows:

801 This listing sucks
802 You've got to be kidding me
803 It's so bad I can't believe it
804 Lovely, simply lovely
805 I just got screwed by another salesman
806 It's a big deal
807 Stop your bitching
808 I didn't design the house. I just listed it
809 You obviously mistook me for another salesman
810 Go pound sand in your fanny
811 An unrealistic price
812 The lawn has ferry rings
813 Exaggeration is not all it's cracked up to be
814 Help me dump this dumb cluck
901 He doesn't have much of a reputation
902 I'm free tonight
903 Can't do better for now

904 I'll give you a ride home
905 Take your time
906 Need a larger deposit
907 Qualify the prospect first
908 Make sure you have the dimensions right
909 It's not a split but a bi-level
910 Hold an Open House on Saturday

Next to the code numbers Ed posted a list of
<u>TEN MOST MISTAKES REALTORS MAKE</u>

- Start their career to late
- Fail to follow up leads
- Cut commissions
- Most realtor's do net set goals
- Underestimate the emotion part in closing a deal
- Underestimate the intelligence of most prospects
- Exaggerate their advertising
- Forget to press their pants/dress
- Can't spell
- Do not wear black socks/pantyhose

By the early 90's being a full-time agent and an investor in 31 rental properties meant Mike had to do a lot of traveling. One summer day he was waiting at the Edmonton International airport for plane to depart to Vancouver when he noticed a computer scale that gave one's weight and fortune for a dollar.

In an effort to make the trip tax deductible as humanly possible Mike dropped a coin into the slot machine and computer screen displayed: "You weigh 175 pounds. You are married. You are on your way to Vancouver."

Ed stood there amazed and after watching three other people step on the scale and their weights, marital status and destination correctly identified, he ran into the men's washroom, changed his clothes put on a pair of dark glasses and stepped on the machine again after dropping a coin.

The computer read: "You still weigh 175 pounds. You are still married. You are on your way to Vancouver. And sir, you have just missed your flight."

When Mike caught the next flight, he was downing a martini as a portly gentleman from Sherwood Park sat beside him ignoring the *No Smoking* sign and while smoking a king-size cigar asked, "Sir, will the smoke bother you, sir?"

"Not if throwing up, won't bother you," Mike replied

The passenger sitting next to Mike put out his cigar but then while flying over the mountains a young boy was making a nuisance out of himself bouncing a ball in the aisle of the jet. Mike became annoyed so he said to the child, "Listen kid, why don't you go outside and play?"

By this time Mike had several more drinks courtesy the airline and when an elderly lady sitting nearby smelled Mike's breath she said to him, "Sir, I think you are going to Hell."

Ed jumped to his feet. "Good heavens!" he said. "I must be on the wrong jet!"

Following his trip to Vancouver Belle and Christian accompanied Mike to one to Toronto for the International Realtors' Convention. Before their flight they each had a bath and a haircut and not to embarrass anyone wore a clean pair of under pants in the event there was a plane crash.

During the flight Mike said to Belle that the real estate business was booming and she could have anything she wanted while he was attending the convention. When the plane arrived at the Pearson International Airport Belle said to her husband, "Mike, darling, that was a wonderful flight. I really enjoyed the plane we were riding in."

Mike purchased the 737 jet on the spot and had Air Canada change the logo to read *Belle Bike's Private Jet*. From this day onward, Belle would have fewer headaches due to carry-on luggage.

To ease the space crunch, found on commercial airlines, Belle wouldn't have to join the frantic scramble for limited overhead storage or have suitcases stuffed in her foot space.

As a frequent traveller Belle wouldn't have to risk back injury trying to hoist heavy suitcases over her head or annoy fellow passengers with a couple of bags and no place to put them.

Best of all, Belle wouldn't have to get her luggage off the carousel, line up when she wanted to use the bathroom or eat cold airline food while 30,000 feet in space.

The following day while watching a baseball game between the Blue Jays and New York Yankees Belle sidled up Mike and said, "The Skydome, a retractable roof, what a beautiful building."

Mike purchased the Skydome outright and as a bonus the CN Tower next to it. Belle now held mortgages on two of the most magnificent buildings in the world.

The following day while shopping at the Eaton Centre Belle said, "Mike, do you think you can buy me a *Mickey Mouse* outfit?"

"Sure thing," Mike replied and purchased his wife the Toronto Maple Leafs of the National Hockey League

The following day the International Realtor's Convention started on time and during a mid-week break Belle and Christian continued shopping and doing a Cultural Difference Survey among Canadian, American, British and Australian realtors.

Mike on the other hand and realtors from India and Israel decided to go into the country and see what other parts of Ontario were like but near Niagara Falls they got caught in a severe thunder storm, visibility became so poor that they couldn't drive another kilometre. Seeing a farmhouse nearby the three tourists asked the farmer to put them up for the night.

"Sure thing," the farmer said and then apologized, "I have a small cabin and there's room only for two. One of you will have to sleep in the barn.'

The realtor from India volunteered but several minutes later he knocked on the cabin door and said to the other two realtors, "I can't stay in the barn because there's a cow inside and to sleep near a cow is against my religion."

"That's all right," said the realtor from Israel. "I'll sleep in the barn."

Minutes later there was a knock on the cabin door and the realtor from Israel said, "I'm story, there's a pig in the barn. That's against my religion."

Mike volunteered but several minutes later there was a knock on the cabin door. The realtor's from India and Israel opened it, and there in front of them stood the cow and the pig. Needless to say the realtor's from India and Israel had little sleep that night. As for Mike he slept well but when he woke up accidentally stepped into two separate manure piles.

As soon as the storm was over the three realtors' after visiting Niagara Falls and St. Catharines too headed back to Toronto where as a highlight of the convention Mike was scheduled to speak about selling real estate in a small market.

As he was about to begin Mike ealized that he had lost his false teeth which embarrassed him.

The convention chairman sitting next to Mike said, "Why don't you try these?"

After trying the pair Mike, frustrated, said, "Too tight."

"I have another pair. Try these."

After trying them on, Mike said, "Too loose."

After trying several more "Try these," mike finally found a pair that fitted perfectly and after a moment's pause began his speech by saying, "It's a pleasure to see you all here tonight at the International Convention of Realtors'—the big shots, the little shots and those who have just come from the cocktail bar, the half—shots."

Following the speech Mike thanked the chairman who helped him during an embarrassing moment. "Thank you for coming to my aid but please tell me, where is your office because while in Toronto I might as well see a dentist."

Mike was surprised when the chairman said, "But I'm not a dentist."

"Who are you then?"

"I'm an undertaker."

The convention concluded with the presentation of "Best Seller Awards" signifying that the realtor in his particular country had sold the most real estate the year before.

The lucky salesman was also privileged to have a photo of the universal insect, the mosquito, used on his calling card.

Records showed that Mike Bike was not only the top realtor in Canada but also Planet Earth and for his efforts was awarded first prize. The prize wasn't an all-expense-two-week holiday for two to Hawaii, Mexico or Disneyland but the opportunity to ask God tree questions.

As soon as technicians made the right connection to Heaven, Ed asked God, "Will I retire a happy man?"

"Yes," replied the Almighty. "But not in your lifetime."

"Will I have a poetry book published?" was Mike's second question.

"Yes, but not while you are on Planet Earth."

Ed's final question was, "Can I become prime minister of Canada?"

"Not in my lifetime God answered. "Why don't you try to become a member of parliament instead?"

"Thank you Lord. Okay, I will," Ed said and did try.

A federal election was announced for October 25 1993 the same month the Toronto Blue Jays won the World Series second year n a row. Joe Carter hit a game winning three-run homer in the bottom of the 9th inning of game 6 defeating the Philadelphia Phillies of the National League.

Mike and Belle were on a flight from Toronto to Edmonton at the time listening to the Series on the radio and as soon the game was over Mike turned his attention to Federal politics and asked Belle if she would be his campaign manager. Belle agreed with two provisos: (1) That should Mike win the election in the constituency of Edmonton North, she would not have to move to Ottawa and (2) That Belle be Mike's ghost writer.

When it came to the latter Mike asked, "Is a ghost writer necessary?"

"Of course," Belle replied and went on to say that approximately 90% of political candidates are lawyers, and that alone makes a ghostwriter necessary.

And that the legal profession has always attracted its share of derision making lawyers spend their entire lives explaining the *past* and thus lacking imagination necessary for a good political speech, which most always hold out a promise for the *future*.

Belle said that by education, training and practice, lawyers were concerned entirely with what has already happened and gave an example if Columbus hadn't had a ghostwriter North America would not have been discovered.

"This is what happened to me' says the client, always in the past tense," Belle said and gave Columbus as an example. "If Columbus had called on a lawyer before embarking on his voyage of discovery, the lawyer would have advised him against making the trip. Columbus's lawyer would have pulled a couple volumes off his shelf and say something like, 'Oh, I have it right here. We need go no further. It's all here.

The statute of the year1178, annotated in the year 1261, part 2, amended in the year 1488 Melendez vs Diaz—the earth is flat and that's that, until new court decisions get into the book'."

After Belle took another breath she continued. "Fortunately Columbus did not see a lawyer. Instead he hired himself a ghost writer who helped fire up the imagination of Queen Isabella and two financial bankers."

At this point Mike said, "Belle, do you want to know something else?"

"What?"

"I'm going to run as an Independent."

"Awesome," Belle said and then asked Mike if he had decided on an election budget?

"I have. It will be $50,000 for printing signs and bumper stickers."

"And the remaining $49,000?"

"For incidentals, Of course these figures are subject to change but the point is that the election is a golden opportunity for me to make international contacts.

"Why so?"

"Should I lose the election Edmonton may name a park after me or I probably end up being a senator, an ambassador to a foreign country and even, perhaps, chairman of the Canadian Broadcasting Corporation."

Why did Mike choose Belle as campaign manager? Several reasons: Often it's not the party that one belongs but the resume of a candidate his/herself, Belle enjoyed wearing multi-coloured dresses signifying Canada is made of many ethnic groups. Belle was in her 50's and going through menopause. As an employee of the *Journal* she knew more about the environment, web sites and surveys than Mike did. And above all Belle having taken care of the lawn at Edbelle Manor and her home, having planted tulip bulbs, pumpkins seeds and pulled up stink weeds, dandelions and grab grass on the acreage was familiar with grass roots which one needs in order to win an election.

As soon as Mike and Belle arrived home and unpacked Mike peeled the floral bed sheets of a giant pumpkin he had grown in the backyard. Tiptoeing around the vines he carefully checked for pumpkin defects.

Then, bending his ear over the nearest gourd, which was has high as his stomach and wider than his Cadillac. Mike gave the pumpkin a sold smack and listened intently like a doctor with a stethoscope.

"This one is thumping pretty well," Mike said to Belle with a grin.

Belle's desire was for Mike to raise a pumpkin larger than anyone else in the neighbourhood.

Mike's enthusiasm has always been to grow a pumpkin larger than the current record at 1.810 pounds and the October weigh-off had begun in Smoky Lake whose festival theme was pumpkins, pumpkins and more pumpkins.

Although extremely busy as a realtor/investor and now involved in federal politics Mike managed to grow a pumpkin that weighed 900 pounds which won him first prize in Smoky Lake.

The prize wasn't an all-paid expense paid trip to Disneyland but one to Nova Scotia where they grow patches and patches of pumpkins and at times the largest in the world.

Ed did not contact NASA or go to Wal-Mart to buy a template which with the right tools one could carve a fantastic face with a wide range of scowling, howling Halloween expressions.

Instead Ed had the University of Alberta engineering students cut a hole in the top for a lid and then slowly, cautiously scoop up the seeds with a spoon, scrape the flesh from inside so the pumpkin shell was an inch thick all the way around thus inventing the first pumpkin canoe in Alberta.

With an oar and a huge sign added, Ed climbed inside and paddled the North Saskatchewan River back and forth urging those with homes facing the river to vote for Mike Bike.

A day later Mike asked Bell, "How did you make out with the Cultural Differences Survey while in Toronto?"

"Fine, just fine," Belle replied. "With Christian's help I noticed there are significant differences between the Americans, Canadians, British and Australians."

"What kind of differences?"

Belle explained the differences this way:

Aussies: Believe you should look out for your mates.

Brits: Believe that you should look out for those who belong to your club.

Americans: Believe that people should look out for and take care of themselves.

Canadians: Believe that it's the government's responsibility.

Aussies: Dislike being mistaken for Pommies (Brits) when abroad.
Canadians: Are indignant about being mistaken for Americans when abroad.
Americans: Encourage being mistaken for Canadians when abroad.
Brits: Can't possibly be mistaken for anyone else when abroad.

Aussies: Are extremely patriotic to their beer.
Americans: Are flag-waving, anthem singing, and obsessively patriotic to the point of blindness.
Canadians: Can't agree on the words to their anthem, when they can be bothered to sing them.
Brits: Don't sing at all but prefer a large brass band to perform the anthem.

Americans: Spend most of their lies glued to the idiot box.
Canadians: Don't, but only because they cant get more American channels.
Brits: Pay a tax just so they can watch four channels.
Aussies: Export all their programs, which no one watches, to Britain, where everyone loves them.

Americans love to watch sports on television.

Brits:	Love to watch sports in stadiums so they can fight with other fans.
Canadians:	Prefer to engage in sports rather than watch them.
Aussies:	Are interested only in swimming, rugby and tennis.

Americans:	Chatter on incessantly about football, baseball and basketball.
Brits:	Chatter incessantly about cricket, soccer and rugby.
Canadians:	Chatter incessantly about hockey, hockey, and hockey.
Aussies:	Chatter on incessantly about how they beat the Brits in every sport.
Americans:	Spell words differently, but still call it "English".
Brits:	Pronounce there words differently, but still call it "English."
Canadians:	Spell like the Brits, pronounce like Americans.
Aussies:	Add "Mate" and a heavy accent to everything they say.

Brits:	Shop at home and have goods imported because they live on an island.
Aussies:	Shop at home and have goods imported because they live on an island.

Americans: Cross the southern border for cheap shopping, gas and liquor in a backwards country.

Canadians: Shop the southern border for cheap shopping, gas and liquor in a wealthy country.

Americans: Drink weak beer.

Canadians: Drink strong beer.

Brits: Drink warm beer.

Aussies: Drink anything with alcohol in it.

Americans: Seem to think that poverty and failure are morally suspect.

Canadians: Seem to believe that wealth and success are morally suspect.

Brits: Seem to believe that wealth, poverty, success and failure are inherited things.

Aussies: Seem to think that none of this matters after several beers.

Canadians: Encourage immigrants to keep their old ways, and avoid assimilation.

Americans: Encourage immigrants to assimilate quickly, and appreciate old ways.

Brits: Encourage immigrants to go to Canada or America.

Aussies: encourage immigrants to stay away.

Canadians: Endure bitterly cold winters, and are proud of it.
Brits: Endure oppressively wet and dreary winters, and are proud of it.
Americans: Don't have to do either and care less.
Aussies: Don't understand what inclement weather means.

Aussies have produced comedians like Paul Hogan and Yahoo Serious.

Canadians have produced comedians, like John Candy, Martin Short, Jim Carrey. Art Linkletter and Dan Akroyd.

Americans: That these people are American.
Brits: Have produced many great comedians, but Americans ignore them.
Brits: Are justifiably proud of the accomplishments of the past citizens.
Americans: Are justifiably proud of the accomplishments of their present citizens.
Canadians: Prattle on how those great Americans were once Canadian.

Aussies: Prattle that many of their citizens at one time were jailbirds.

Mike was delighted with Cultural Difference Survey Belle had done. The finer points could be used during the upcoming election."

CHAPTER 7

After weathering a cool autumn Ed approached the election at 62 years of age and Belle was 59. The major concerns in the Edmonton at the time can best be described in three words: Sudden Exploding Fish in the North Saskatchewan River. At least voters should have expressed concern because aside from having a grass fire at one of its parameters, through carelessness of some kind or another, one of Edmonton's premier tourist attractions had been badly trashed because of exploding fish. Emontonians were literally weeping over this, a phenomenon that took place most often just before sunrise.

One fisherman gave an account of such an explosion in the *Examiner.* Next to the article was a photo of a pike which had a large gouged hole in the middle. The fish could have been a star in a low-budgeted horror movie entitled *Fish in Jeopardy*.

Unknown to the public however, there was speculation that rival Calgary had something to do with the catastrophe.

As a formally declared candidate Mike was familiar with the sights and sounds of the constituency and to anyone who cared to listen said, "I intend to be upright, honest and straightforward during my election campaign. You won't see me slinging mud at anyone. I state that my number one priority is to find out what is causing the fish to explode in the North Saskatchewan River and I'm assigning my wife Belle, to do a study. The rest of my platform will be unveiled to the media tomorrow."

The following day Mike held a media news conference and released his ten-point platform.

1. Do a study of fish exploding in the North Saskatchewan River.
2. Make Pig Latin the third national language in Canada.
3. Have a pumpkin replace the maple leaf on the Canadian flag.
4. Have the beaver removed as a symbol of Canada
5. Make *Auld Lang Syne* the national anthem of the human race.
6. Valentine's Day would be moved to February 29th so it would only occur in leap years.
7. Establish an oil refinery in Edmonton instead of Texas
8. Have senators elected.
9. Help Edmonton to get a new hockey arena and a museum.
10. Make the dandelion Canada's national flower.

At the conclusion of the news conference Mike said, "It deeply concerns me that none of the other potential candidates has the courage to speak on the daily fish explosion or the other subjects such as a new hockey arena in Edmonton, I'm going to push forward."

Why did Mike run as an Independent aside from his interest in the environment? Because of his disenchantment with the old-line parties. When Ed first voted Liberal and then Conservative both parties seemed to him no different from the other and MP's on both sides of the House of Commons made derogatory remarks during *Question Period*.

Mike never believed in Socialism so he had nothing to do with the New Democratic Party.

There were gaffes in the campaign, some funny and some fatal.

Then there was the time Mike spoke to the Edmonton Women's Equal Rights Movement and did not follow the script Belle had written and said to the ladies present, "Women unite! Because I'll be candid with you, if you are split down the middle you'll always find men on top of you."

Next day Mike visited a cheese factory, even put on a silly-looking hygienic cap, only to find out that, oops, the factory owner did not support Mike's view on unpasteurized cheese.

Then there was the time the Edmonton undertaker, Alvin Smith who went to file his nomination papers at deadline as the New Democratic candidate but found he hadn't bothered to become a Canadian citizen.

But the Conservative Party too distinguished itself with triple play gaffes. There was the early revelation that their star candidate Archibald Cheat, as a lawyer, defended a hatemonger that believed there was no Holocaust and people wondered as soon as he announced his candidacy, "What is there for him? All we need is another lawyer in Ottawa to screw things up."

Then card carrying Conservatives came forward to link Cheat to a neo-Nazi group and forced to leave the Conservative Party.

Conservative officials then blatantly admitted they knew about Cheat's right-wing views before an article appeared in the *Sun* but decided not to tell the Conservative leader who was Kim Campbell the Prime Minister at the time.

Then with the deadline-approaching lawyer Paul "Boomer" Cross won the candidacy but next day was charged with overcharging Legal Aid. Hearing this Prime Minister Campbell stepped in and fired Cross as the party's candidate.

"The Prime Minister is one to talk about corruption, graft and awarding contracts to friends," Cross said publicly and ungraciously refused to withdraw his candidacy.

The Prime Minister then ordered the riding Association to pick another individual, which it did.

It picked Cross's campaign manager but in the end she refused to file her nomination papers by deadline and Cross ran as an Independent. Edmonton North now had two Independent candidates, Paul "Boomer" Cross and Michael Bike.

The Conservatives had no candidate but Cross's people pulled several boners too.

They warned voters through newspaper and radio ads that if Liberal government were elected voters in Edmonton would have to pay a large amount of taxes and sent out tax notices to all constituency homes, including apartment dwellers.

The unsubstantiated claims came in business envelopes with *NOTICE OF ASSESSMENT* printed on them. The claim was that over the next five years Liberal programs would cost individual taxpayers in Canada in excess of $2,000 per person.

There was a P. S. on the notice which in part read: "Just think how many Big Mac's you could get for that amount of money."

Unfortunately for the Cross group the Provincial Assessment Authority had just mailed out the *real* notices.

And Pastor Taylor of the No Name Universal Church pulled a faux pas too when in his Sunday service said, ". . . it's time for some change."

Hearing the pastor all the Liberals, except those with sore knees, walked out vowing not to go to church until Reverend Taylor apologized and even then, they would put slugs into the collection basket instead of coins.

The difference in Edmonton North politics, compared to the rest of Canada, was that there were 2 Independent candidates, an incumbent Liberal, and no New Democratic Party candidate in a country governed by right-wing Conservatives.

The Liberal Les "Speed" Westgate was a sitting member of the House of Commons for 16 years and an experienced politician even if he wasn't sitting but standing up. Although Liberals called him, "The old work horse." Cross supporters called him, "A jackass and a womanizer."

Westgate owned a motel in Edmonton along that had a restaurant attached to it. That of course isn't saying a great deal. He also owned other motels and restaurants throughout North Central Alberta but lost them when he failed to make mortgage payments on them.

Then Belle did some nosing around and what she discovered about Westgate surprised Mike. Besides having several motels and restaurants foreclosed on Belle found that:

1. When the Liberals were in power Westgate was going to be named Canada's foreign minister but the appointment wasn't made because he couldn't speak French.
2. Westgate tried marijuana while attending High School.
3. Westgate never had an inclination to attend the annual Heritage Day Festival although he enjoyed taking part in ribbon-cutting ceremonies.
4. Westgate constantly complained about the courts, parole boards, universities, the feminist movement and continually protested Wal-Mart.
5. Westgate employed an alien nanny from Jamaica.
6. Westgate fabricated the number of times he stood in the House of Commons to speak.

Then Belle did a similar expose on Paul "Boomer" Cross. Belle's findings showed, aside from over-charging Legal Aid he was:

1. Left-handed putting him in the same fraternity as Napoleon Bonaparte and Jack the Ripper.
2. As a youngster Cross put pepper in a cheerleader's pom-pom.
3. Cross had a joint bank account. A deposit account for his wife and a chequeing one for himself.
4. When Cross had a frog in his mouth it was probably the first piece of meat he had in weeks.
5. As a youngster Cross killed a Canada goose in Hawrelak Park with a slingshot.
6. Cross was a charter member of the *I Hate Ketchup Club of Canada*.

Halfway through the election campaign Mike went up and down Edmonton North constituency streets shaking hands, kissing babies and handing out cigars. Following this ritual he would go to his campaign headquarters, close the door behind him and discuss strategy with his campaign manager where one day Mike said, "I'm not as young as I use to be but still my only concern in this election is that Cross and Westgate are going to lose their deposits."

While Westgate and Cross were planning their campaign strategies Belle lined up a series of appearances for her husband which included a constituency High School graduating class where Mike said, "Education is great and High School sex is dandy. Belle's survey shows however, that four out of five high school students still prefer candy. And before you enjoy that candy make sure you do your homework. And no matter what career you choose, you aren't going to be successful if you have a stupid haircut, a tattoo or body piercing ring in your nose."

The High School students were greatly impressed with Ed's speech. This was confirmed by the questions they asked afterward: "Why can't scientists make birth control retroactive?" "While walking why, in most instances is the right foot at a 100 degree angle?" "Do ants sleep?" "Does tobacco cause cancer?" and, "Which contains more caffeine, *Pepsi* or *Coke*?"

And then one student, louder than the rest asked, "Sir, do you know any lawyer jokes?"

"I do," Mike replied and told the story of how Judge Brian Black couldn't make it as a lawyer so he got an appointment as a judge. "That's the greatest joke in our present society."

The following day Mike spoke to students at MacEwan College and as a guest speaker spoke on the subject of steroids and Abuse of Drugs and Alcohol. Ed began by saying, "Suppose I had a pail of water and some of my home-brewed beer on this stage, and then brought in a donkey, which of the two you think the donkey would choose?"

"The donkey would take the water!" a student from the back hollered. "How did you reach that conclusion?"

"Because the donkey is an ass!" the student replied and Ed left it at that.

Like at the High School students at MacEwan College were greatly impressed with Ed's speech. This was shown by the questions they asked afterward, several of which were:

"What language is spoken by French Canadians?" "Why do scientists use rats instead of lawyers for laboratory experiments?" "Mr. Bike, who do you prefer, the Rolling Stones or the Beatles?" and, Which book should be compulsory reading in the Physiology curriculum: *The Origin and Growth of Whiskers* or *Hair and its Destruction?"*

Mike was accompanied to the College by a reporter from the *Sun* who wrote an article about Mike that he brewed his own beer and may not have a proper license to do so.

When Mike read he article he said to Belle, "This is another example of media's desire to dig up sensational dirt about me."

Belle nodded her head as Mike continued, "Of course I expect this kind of scrutiny. We live in an age where voters' do not believe politicians or the media. Voters believe half of the legislators are crooks."

You better retract that statement," Belle said. "Not half are crooks."

"Okay." Mike said. "Voters feel half of the legislators are not crooks. However, I must condition myself to have dirty laundry aired in public. I admit for example, to have made mistakes in my lifetime, such as fishing in the North Saskatchewan River without a license and not paying a traffic fine after I went through a *STOP* sign recently. But this is water under the bridge and while St. Patrick may have killed all the snakes in Ireland, I say it's time to get rid of all the baboons in Ottawa. Now is the time to get on the Mike Bike bandwagon."

While returning home after a hectic day of campaigning Mike was stopped by police at a *CHECK STOP* and hauled into police headquarters where he paid for a previous traffic violation. The following day Belle handed Mike a copy of the *Sun* where on the front page he read the banner headline *Independent MP Candidate Mike* Bike *Arrested*.

It seems local police in a crackdown of traffic violations, issued hundreds of warrants. Ed had neglected to pay a fine for going through a *STOP* sign while campaigning. Ed paid the $100 fine and was released. Police had earlier warned anyone with traffic violation tickets to pay their penalty immediately or be arrested at home or at work.

"I admit it's embarrassing," Mike said to Belle after he finished reading the article, "But it shouldn't influence people who may have voted for me."

"Why so?" Belle said.

"Because I don't know of an adult driver who hasn't received a traffic violation ticket in his or her lifetime."

Election time was an exciting event in Edmonton where each of the candidates had handbills printed and distributed, 4 X 8 plywood signs placed at strategic locations and Vote For . . . signs on lawns, fences and buildings.

There were car bumper stickers too, several of which read: *DON'T TRUST A POLITICIAN! NO MORE POLITICAL PATRONAGE!* And *WHY WASTE YOUR VOTE?*

By now Mike felt his chances of winning the election were increasing. This occurred at election headquarters where Mike planned strategy with three doctors—rookie, one in the mid 40's, and one about to retire.

The four were discussing Mike's rivals when the rookie said, "From experience the best patient to operate on are computer scientists. One can open them up, everything is colour coded. You can easily find out what you need and remove or repair it."

Then the middle-aged practioner said, "Once you get to be my age in life, and you have the biggest challenge behind you, you must restrict you practice to civil engineers. Once you open them up, you find something that everything is labelled, chrome-plated and has screw fastenings. It's a piece of cake to find a defective part, remove it and replace it."

The doctor about to retire said, "By the time you get to be my age in life you want no challenges at all. You must mark time and money until retirement. I restrict my practice to surgery of lawyers. Once you open them up they have only two parts, a mouth and an asshole and they are interchangeable."

Mike could not restrain himself any longer from saying. "Mouth" and "Asshole." Hey! That describes Paul "Boomer" Cross and Les "Speed" Westgate perfectly."

Following the strategy meeting Mike returned home, sank into a comfortable chair and said to Belle, "Honey, the campaign is going fine. I now believe I can sweep the constituency."

Belle, who was working on a report why fish were exploding in the North Saskatchewan River, looked at her husband wearily. "Great," she said. "Then why don't you grab the broom and start with the living room?"

After Mike swept the living room he asked Belle how her Fish Study was coming along.

"Fine, I think hot flashes during menopause have something to do with the explosions."

"You mean to say fish go through a menopause?"

"That's still being researched."

Mikewas worrying about the subject too because Belle was experiencing menopause, was at times cantankerous, and he had read that there were 3.5 million women in Canada over fifty and that the number was expected to top 5-million by the year 2015 when more women would be experiencing menopause than any time in Canadian history.

"Just think. If all that heat is concentrated at one time at one point, say Edmonton, what a big explosion that would be, "Mike said.

Belle nodded her head and then sparing no expense interviewed Rabbi Libowitch's wife who confined that menopause indeed could have an effect on global warming and cause fish to explode. "Personally at the moment I can cover either polar cap with steam," she said.

This seemed fairly conclusive having come from the wife of a rabbi but with a problem of this magnitude Belle had to have other input so she phoned a friend in India whom she got to know during the International Realtors' Convention when it was held in Toronto, and spoke to her husband. The husband said, quote, "Mahzabeen is going through menopause now, and believe me it's not pretty.

The temperature at a lake near Calcutta has gone up five degrees since she and other women her age had power surges at the same time. Who knows, maybe the same thing is happening in Edmonton."

After interviewing menopause authorities in Mexico City, Cairo and Manila Belle's study still wasn't conclusive so she rented a mini-submarine, like the one, which found the *Titanic*, and along with a scientist from the University of Alberta traversed the bottom of the river. Dr. Abe Sigler called this back and forth routine, "A bold new age in river exploration."

Of course the scientist could say that but Belle couldn't because the criss-crossing, back and forth, made her dizzy.

When Belle recovered from the dizziness the mini-submarine was at the bottom of the river where the couple collected soil and water samples along with mercury teeth fillings and articles to numerous to mention all in pursuit of exploring the knowledge of climate and pollution and the effect both had on fish in the City of Champions.

There were a plethora of reasons based not only on a religious belief why the fish suddenly kept exploding but also that as soon as the fish were cut open a concentration of human and toxic waste was found inside the fish tissue. It seems that roughly 1.5 billion litters of partly treated effluent had spilled into the North Saskatchewan River from the city treatment plant and officials had no idea how to solve the problem and had not shown a sense of urgency to fix the problem.

The other theory was that because a sanitary shortage of public toilets during the Fishing Derby fishermen, especially from foreign countries, in order to relieve themselves at a portable lavatory instead used the river to dispose their waste which combined with the mercury and magnesium from natural sources were the exploding culprit. Both theories however, were inconclusive.

Belle said she witnessed a similar explosion when she lived on the farm with her parents. "At that time I watched a cow explode after the animal had eaten alfalfa."

With that conclusion Belle handed her report to Ed who several days later at an election rally said, "Friends. Not only is the North Saskatchewan River in peril, so is the Athabasca near Fort McMurray where the fish are dying along with the Canada geese and ducks."

A week before the election the three candidates appeared at a public forum sponsored by the Chamber of Commerce. Numbers were drawn from a hat as to which candidate would speak first, second and third.

Westgate spoke first and fought to win the Edmonton North seat in the House of Commons based on past experience and to serve Edmonton, Canada and hockey.

Westgate also begged the electorates not no judge him on the past record of other politicians whose actions he could not control, especially the contracts that were doled out to relatives, friends, and companies that contributed to the election campaign. And above all, the secrecy behind the appointment of senators and judges.

Cross during his to speech accused Westgate of false promises and slammed what he termed, "Lies and innuendos."

Cross then spoke about the enormous spruce tree he had grown in his back yard and promised to work diligently to make Edmonton the oil capital of Canada.

Then in an emotional part of the speech Cross urged voters not to waste their ballot on either Westgate or Bike because a recent poll he had taken showed that he was the most popular candidate.

When it was Mike's turn to speak he took exception to the poll Cross had taken and said, "Choice is of paramount concern to the voters. The survey you conducted may be rife with bias. My poll will be released tomorrow."

Initially Mike felt that both Westgate and Cross were impressive orators and formidable candidates and it appeared like a two-way fight between Westgate and Cross to win the election.

This down feeling changed, however, when Ed continued his speech and turning to Cross and pointing his finger said, "You, sir are a political plum, the result of careful grafting. Your political machine is well oiled and it's no wander your group of supporters have so much friction."

Ed's assessment of the two opponents must have struck favour with the voters because after the forum Belle's poll showed Ed's popularity rising with leaps and bounds. "There is a surge, an uprising, groundswell," Belle went on to describe her latest poll, which appeared in the *Examiner* and was 19 out of 20 times correct and had a margin of error of 4.5 percent.

Then came the weekend before the election date. Mike's excitement about being the next MP was short lived when Westgate leaked a report to the media, true or false, that he was carrying the constituency. How Westgate could carry such a large parcel of land is difficult to understand but Westgate did say, "Belle Bike is plumb wrong with her survey. Survey's are for losers."

What Paul "Boomer" Cross said at the time was that he had to cancel a radio interview because of recurring laryngitis. "Why my vocal cords aren't working as well as Westgate's or Bike's is because I'm answering questions and they aren't."

Finally came the great day itself where at this juncture Mike's volunteers phoned each household on the polling list reminding them, "Vote for Mike Bike."

When the polling stations closed at 8:00 p. m. many of Mike's supporters were still inside casting their ballots. Many had forsaken their nightly chores, taking daughters to a ballet lesson and sons to either Little League baseball or soccer games.

Mike, Belle and strategists watched returns come in at campaign headquarters by watching television and listening to the radio at the same time.

While the Conservatives were winning federally, in the Edmonton North riding a three-way race developed. First Westgate was in the lead, then Cross and then Mike.

In the next bulletin Cross was in the lead, Mike second and Westgate third. The three candidates kept changing positions as often as Best Realty had new salesmen. This lasted for three hours until the Returning Officer finally declared; "Mike Bike wins the election with a plurality of 1200 votes. A recount is unnecessary."

Here's a scoop on Mike's election. Both Westgate and Cross said after the ballots were counted, why Mike Bike won the election, was due to a full moon on the day the election was held.

"People were under a full moon spell and voted like zombies," Westgate said. What Cross said was, "Why I lost is because Edmonton was without bus service due to a strike by the drivers."

At any rate one should have been at the Crowne Plaza Hotel ballroom that night when Mike and Belle walked inside and a five-piece band struck up the tune *For he's a jolly good fellow*. After Mike beaming and supporters cheering, gave his *Thank You* speech he pumped his fists in to the air and said, "Friends, it's time to boogie."

Mike then grabbed Belle by arm and the couple took to the dance floor. Soon a keg of Mike's home-brewed beer was opened to the burst of applause. Then many of those who voted against Mike joined those who did. Several came up to Mike saying that they weren't Conservatives, Liberals or members of the New Democratic Party but Reformers.

Even undertaker Alvin Smith came up congratulates Mike and said his conscience was bothering him because although he couldn't vote he had licked envelopes for Westgate.

Smith wondered if his wife could get the job as the next census taker.

To others who reminded Mike that it was only in the last minute that they decided to vote for him and wanted a job Ed had a standard reply which was, "I had to kiss your ass so you would vote for me, now you can kiss mine if you want me to find you employment."

From then on Mike said nothing. Now that he was an elected member of parliament he didn't have to say much, aside from his maiden speech. For the next 4 or 5 years MP Mike Bike didn't have to say a word enjoying numerous perks and free airfare from Edmonton to Ottawa and vice versa.

The alternate plan for Mike could be is to suck up to the Prime Minister and get an appointment to the senate or an ambassadorship to a foreign country. At any rate Ed winning the election was one of his greatest triumphs because if he won another election he was entitled to a lucrative pension.

CHAPTER 8

In Ottawa the back wall of Mike's office had shelves with books. Behind his desk were flags of Canada and Alberta. Near his desk stood an aquarium filled with North Saskatchewan River fish at one end and a pumpkin at the other.

It was a week after Mike got elected that he attended the *New MP School* that outlined the rules and procedures to follow while in the House of Commons and have a TV camera zoomed on him during *Question Period.*

Another week elapsed before Mike began receiving mail and requests to be a guest speaker. He all ready received copies of the *Journal* and the *Sun* that were two weeks late. Mike also began to receive mail from lobbying groups along with pens, calendars, ashtrays and coffee mugs with logos on them.

During the third week in Ottawa there was no hoopla, no buttons, no posters or bumper stickers but plenty of pomp and circumstance as the Governor General opened a new session of parliament and later Mike made his maiden speech. Mike did not speak about maidens, however, but asked questions what the Federal Government was going to do about the exploding fish in the North Saskatchewan River now that the city of Edmonton seemed to be in an environmental peril?

After Mike handed the Speaker of the House of Commons a copy of Belle's report he with head tilted back, arms akimbo, eyes wide, tonsils flapping asked other questions too, several of which were:

"When will Pig Latin become the third official language in Canada? Isn't it time to replace the maple leaf on the Canadian flag with a pumpkin? And when will Christmas shopping become an Olympic event?"

At the end of his speech Mike, who interjected the phrase "Mr. Speaker" after every second sentence, invited all the MP's to spend their next summer holidays in Edmonton.

When Mike returned to his office his secretary, Madam Bouchard, reminded the new MP to send a newsletter to his constituents. She said, "It won't cost you a penny and leave an impression back home that you are extremely busy."

After Mike and Madam Bouchard discussed the format of the newsletter she handed Mike the mail and together they went through the letters. One letter invited Mike to St. John's, Newfoundland because fish in Newfoundland were exploding also.

Another letter came from B'na Brith in Toronto question Mike if he preferred muffins to bagels. Next there was a letter addressed simply to "*The Stupidest MP in Canada.*"

"One would get angry even before it's opened," Madam Bouchard said.

"Oh," replied MP Mike, "I wouldn't get angry over a letter like that but it does upset me when I realize the Post Office knew where to deliver it."

Mike also received a chain letter. He thought the letter was a joke until he read, "If you break this chain, calamity will strike you. You will end up in a hospital, warts as big as cauliflowers will sprout on your face. Your friends will avoid you. Eventually you will die in a swimming pool and meet St. Peter at the Pearly Gates."

The chain letter was signed by the Edmonton medium whom Ed slapped her face when he was a rookie real estate salesman.

After Madam Bouchard said that Mike should ignore the chain letter he said, "Madam Bouchard, you are as wise as an owl."

"After thirty years in this business one gets to know little tricks," Madam Bouchard said and then asked, "How do you feel about compulsory retirement at the age of sixty-five?"

"Canadian judges, who make important decisions, work until they are 75. Why can't anyone else?" Mike said.

"I'm glad you feel that way."

"Why?"

"Because I'm 64, and if you want me to be your secretary next year, you better convince your colleagues on Parliament Hill to change the existing law."

After several months in Ottawa Ed began receiving frequent mail from his own constituency. He enjoyed reading several in particular. The first was from Edmonton *Meals on Wheels* who wanted Ed to become honorary chairman during a campaign to raise funds renovating its kitchen.

The second letter was from Belle who instead of coming to Ottawa with her husband decided to stay in Edmonton even though she owned a private jet, and have a friend, Dominic, live with her.

When Ed opened another letter the signature was difficult to read but after putting it under a magnifying glass he deciphered that it came from the ghost whose head caught on fire while being a goalie for the Edmonton junior Kings Hockey team. In his letter the ghost applied for federal funding in order to build a monument honouring the goats that died in Edmonton during the past century and also help Belle build a monument marking the death of three witches who were hanged in Edmonton in the year 1892.

Mike was opposed to such monuments but hoping the ghost would vote for him in the next election, passed on the request to a committee which looked after federal funding.

As soon as Mike was done going through his mail he rushed to the Canadian Archives in Ottawa and read up on the witch hangings and indeed found artefacts and literature about, "Witches of Edmonton."

Twenty-five years later, according to information left with the Archives, the minister of Justice at the time addressed his townspeople, "History imposes us tonight a delicate balance and a difficult task. We are here to commemorate something we would be willing to forget."

The residents of Edmonton long absorbed the shock which had sent three innocent Christians, including Bell's grand, grandparents, to hang on the gallows in 1892 and hoped the incident would have been forgotten and it was, until the ghost which Mike planted in his backyard and later became a goaltender for the Edmonton Oil Kings hockey team, revived it.

To this point in time anthropologists still hadn't found why the ghosts head burst into flames when he was hit by a puck following slap shot by a defenseman from the Medicine Hat Tigers. One anthropologist said however, that with a hockey team named Kings there could have been gunpowder placed inside the puck or the Medicine Hat team was against monarchy.

As recently as the time the Edmonton Oilers\s won their first Stanley Cup the Winter family petitioned the Alberta Government to declare the witches innocent. The lawmakers passed an inconclusive resolution declaring, "The terrible way the ancestors were treated may have been tried illegally under the shocking laws of the time, and their defendants should harbour no feeling of guilt or shame."

Such stories are never forgotten, however, and when the ghost heard about the hangings he also wanted to make *Witchcraft* a cottage industry in Edmonton and to build not only a ghost monument but also another to remember the three witches.

Initially the Edmonton Chamber of Commerce supported the idea and while anticipating a government grant, members ordered new stationery, purchased hats and were taking lessons from a high Witch priest on how to properly fly on a broomstick from one place to another. The high priest demanded that the brush part should be in the front part of the broom and not the back as some Chamber members were seen flying during practice. Several businessmen were switching their address to read Edmonton *Witchville* but don't come to Edmonton to see a witch monument in the community.

The committee which handled the ghost's request for funding thought it was a great idea but when the application got into the hands of the Federal Minister of Finance, he turned down the request saying, "Canada must reduce its deficit. Our national budget is so out of whack already that the Yanks are watching us."

In the end the ghost created the monuments himself. The full-scale statue of two Puritan women and a man obviously suffering was presented to the City Council and accepted. The mayor at the time, however, vetoed the acceptance. Council overrode the veto. A flurry of debates ensued. Eventually council voted to deny the request.

Finally the ghost took the ghost monument and placed it in a park at the north end of Edmonton but when the first heavy rain came, the plaster dissolved and floated away into the North Saskatchewan River.

In a weeks time all those who changed names to Edmonton *Witchville* changed them back simply to Edmonton except Rabbi Abe Libowitch who always kept his original name. As for Belle, she fell madly in love with a long-lost friend with a name Dominic.

Despite Ed living in Ottawa and Belle in Edmonton with Dominic Mike's and Belle's relationship was excellent and unfaltering. Belle spent much of her time entertaining Dominic but there were days too when she entertained her neighbours.

One evening Belle, Lisa and Edna met at the Westin Hotel bar and while sipping on a cocktail discussed their respective husbands.

Lisa was an immensely loveable character who went prematurely grey so she dyed her hair a range of festive colours. This particular evening she was a copper blond. Lisa always smelled exotic, not because of the under arm deodorant she used but a combination of expensive perfume and cigarette smoke.

Edna on the other hand had a knack of making people feel as if one had known her for ever. She always wore fashionable clothing, knew the latest dance step and how to play the piano and guitar but never attended a Rock concert. Edna was a blond and bubbly.

After a second round of cocktails Lisa said, "My husband is fantastic. For my birthday he bought me a mink coat."

"And mine, for my birthday bought me a yacht." Edna said.

Then Belle said, "Since Ed became a member of parliament he's so busy that he forgot to buy me anything and his tummy has grown so large that 300 cockroaches can stand on it side by side."

After a long silence Lisa said, "Listen girls, I was lying. My husband didn't buy me fur coat but one made out of cloth."

Edna followed, "Well, since you are telling the truth, Lisa, you might as well know that my husband didn't buy me a yacht but a rowboat."

Lisa and Edna stared at each other when Belle cut in and said, "Okay, okay, so I will tell the truth too. That part about the 300 cockroaches standing side by side on my husband's stomach isn't true. The 299th cockroach had to stand on only one leg."

The following Saturday night Belle, Lisa and Edna were enjoying cocktails at the Westin Hotel Bar again but this time they were trying to impress each other how much money their husband's made.

"My husband just bought me a necklace and an earring set for our wedding anniversary, which cost $25,000, but I had to return it because I'm allergic to platinum," Lisa said.

"I understand exactly what you mean," Edna continued.

"For our wedding anniversary my husband bought me a mink coat but I had to return it because I'm allergic to fur."

Just then Belle fainted. Her glass fell to the floor. When she recovered Lisa and Edna asked what made her faint.

Belle sighed, "I guess I'm allergic to hot air."

Despite living separately Mike and Belle did exchange gifts. At first they were going to climb inside a box and mail themselves to each other but Canada Post employees went on strike for higher wages so that plan did not work.

To mark their wedding anniversary Mike went to a jewellery store in Ottawa. Seeing a musical box, which wound up played the tune *I Love You Truly* Ed said to the clerk, "That's a gift my wife in Edmonton will like but for one thing, Belle doesn't like the colour blue."

"No problem," the clerk said. "We have some that are red in colour," and wrapped the musical jewellery box with appropriate paper.

The day the gift arrived in Edmonton Belle was ecstatic until she unwrapped the jewellery box and it began playing *The Old Gray Mare Ain't What She Used To Be*.

Belle wasn't perfect when it came to choosing gifts either. For a birthday gift for Mike she went to the *Hudson's Bay* store and said to the saleslady, "I'd like to buy a hat for my husband who is in Ottawa."

"Certainly, "said the clerk and asked what size.

"I think Ed takes size seventeen."

"Seventeen?" gasped the clerk. "You must be mistaken. Hats don't come in that size."

"Don't tell me that," Belle said, "I didn't marry a freak of nature but a realtor who turned to be a politician. I know Ed's shirt collar is size 15 and his head is certainly larger than his neck."

By the time Belle purchased the right-sized hat and sent it away, it was nighttime. As soon as Belle returned home she crawled into bed with Dominic. As Belle gazed at Dominic she remembered that it wasn't his looks that attracted her to Dominic when she first met him. It was at the Days Inn Hotel bar that Belle came alone, sat on a stool and found out that Dominic had replaced Pumpkin as a security guard at the hotel.

As soon as Dominic spotted Belle he leapt from behind a counter and sat on a vacant stool next to her. Dominic didn't offer to buy Belle a drink but after one glance in Belle's direction, she did not suggest he was an unacceptable replacement for Ed

A minute later Dominic planted a kiss on Belle's cheek and she returned the touch with a smile. Neither Belle nor Dominic felt the need to speak and sat in silence, each thinking what would happen next. Belle kept drinking her cocktail and Dominic his milk.

When the bartender cried out," Last call! We're closing in the next half-hour!" Belle and Dominic jumped into a car and left together for home where Dominic envied Belle whose hair was turning grey and who still was riding a mechanical bull each day as an exercise routine.

Belle never questioned Dominic's background but the truth must be known since Dominic came from a large family and eventually became an orphan. Dominic began to drift, often trying to stay ahead of the law, which was difficult to do in those days.

Eventually Dominic showed up at the Days *Inn* Hotel in Edmonton and hired as a security guard.

All Dominic wanted in life was someone to love, regular food and perhaps a family of his own. And so that night Belle allowed Dominic to sleep in the same bed as she did. This led to a second night, and a third, until they discovered that they really loved each other and even Ed's return from Ottawa would not break them apart.

By loving Dominic Belle wasn't breaking rules in contemporary society, even when he attempts to commit adultery with all the *D's* in the Edmonton telephone directory.

Dominic can anticipate almost to the second when Belle will have breakfast ready for him. First he hears the sound of milk pouring into a bowel and Belle hollers, "Hey, Dominic, my pet! It's time for breakfast!"

At that point Dominic heads straight for the kitchen where Belle says, "Good morning, Dominic."

As Dominic walks closer to Belle she pushes the bowl towards him and then, Dominic begins to lap the milk happily and the same time wagging his tail from side to side.

It's a myth that a German shepherd dog lost may not eventually find his rightful owner. It's a myth too that male newspaper columnists are more widely read than female columnists. Belle's weekly column *Ask Belle* in the *Journal* was so popular that it was syndicated and carried by other newspapers throughout Canada.

Being a farmer's daughter, married to a wealthy realtor who became a politician, a landlord who owned her own private aircraft, and naturally because of her age, Belle Bike was well qualified to comment on social, economic, political and moral issues facing Planet Earth in turbulent days. Belle's column was popular mainly on the strength of her profound responses to questions submitted by her readers. Here's a sample of an *Ask Belle* column in a Sunday edition of the *Journal.*

> Dear Belle:
> I just read in a Regina newspaper that in Saskatchewan there was a dust storm recently where gophers were seen digging holes 50 feet in the air. I want the truth. Is this possible?
>
> Fred
>
> Dear Fred:
> It's the truth. I had the experience of traveling through that storm and saw gophers digging holes 50 feet in the air. Not only did I see gophers but also prior to the storm grasshoppers were so huge that farmers flipped them upside down and used the hoppers as hayracks.
> Dear Belle:
>
> I gave my landlord a verbal notice on the 17th of the month that I'm terminating my rental agreement. Can the landlord hold me responsible for another months rent?
>
> Nimfa

Dear Nimfa:

Your intention not to occupy the suite must be (1) in writing and (2) given to the landlord on the last or first day of the month. Yes, you are stuck with paying another months rent.

Dear Belle:

I'm planning a holiday in the Okanagan valley of British Columbia where there are rattlesnakes. I have read in a book that when one meets a rattlesnake to stand absolutely still and look the snake in the eyes. The snake will rattle its tail and slither away. Is that true?

Vernon

Dear Vernon:

You may have read the book but has the snake? If you find out, please write me.

Dear Belle:

I recently went to the Calgary zoo to see the monkeys but the cute little things were mating. I asked the attendant if they would come out of the cave if I gave them a peanut but they wouldn't. Any idea why?

Rita

Dear Rita:

Put yourself in the monkey's place. Would you?

Dear Belle:
My wife is suspicious that I'm running around with another woman. For instance, last night she asked if it was Betty Brown at the Post office, Shirley Janko at the IGA Store, or Carol Bamm, the nurse at the hospital. What should I do?

Bill

Dear Bill:
Cheer up. You may not be fooling around but your wife certainly gave you three good leads to get something going.

Dear Belle:
I recently bought a Canada Savings bond and presented it to the clerk. She asked me if I wanted the bond converted or redeemed. What did she mean?

Jim

Dear Jim:
I'm not certain. It depends if the clerk you dealt with was a bank or a church.

Dear Belle:
Can you please tell me how many employees is there at Best Realty broken down by sex?

Herman

Dear Herman:
I checked with my husband, Ed, and he tells me not many. Liquor is more of a problem.

Dear Belle:
I'm a High School student in Winnipeg studying Environment. In your opinion, what is the greatest threat to Planet Mother Earth?

Roger

Dear Roger:
I went at great expense to come up with an answer. After speaking to your mother I have concluded that it's your bedroom.

Dear Belle:
I have received my first pay cheque and spent it all on clothing. My boyfriend urges me to put the money into a savings account instead. He argues that thrift is a virtue but I insist clothing makes women. Can you help me decided what to do—put my money into more clothing or in a bank account?

Tessie

Dear Tessie:
Put your money into whichever draws the most interest.

Dear Belle:
Last week I had fish for dinner at a restaurant that I shall not mention, but the fish didn't look good. What should I do, tell the owner?

Ralph

Dear Ralph:
I know several things about etiquette ever since Emily Post was a stump. I wouldn't mention the fish you ate to anyone. If you were dead as long as the fish, you wouldn't look good either.

CHAPTER 9

As soon as the House of Commons adjourned for the summer holidays Mike returned home where he visited as many of his constituents as he could but his personality had changed. Mike kept wearing a hat to cover his bald spot and developed a large belly from the cases and cases of his home-brew beer he had taken with him to Ottawa.

One of the first people Mike met was the lady in charge of *Meals on Wheels*, Anita Pander, and said to her, "How is campaign for funds coming?"

"Great," Mrs. Pander said. "The building is built but we still need equipment for the kitchen."

"And what will the equipment cost?'

"Approximately $20,000."

"I'll tell you something," Mike said. "To raise $20,000 in Edmonton isn't easy these days. Why don't you put on a meal and the public roast me?"

"Mike that's and excellent idea. I'll speak to my cooks and have the tickets printed right away. On what date do you suggest the roast be held?"

Mike looked at a calendar, which he always carried in his wallet and after studying the optional dates said, "How about next Saturday?"

"Fine, I'll have a committee start planning right away."

In the meantime M P Mike continued visiting his constituents and went to his bank to cash a cheque. Not seeing Ed for some time the teller said, "Could you please identify yourself?"

"Sure can. Is there a mirror around?'

"Mirror? Oh, yes, on the post behind you."

Mike glanced at the mirror and heaved a sigh of relief. "Yeah," he said. "I'm Mike Bike the Member of Parliament for Edmonton North."

The teller still refused to cash the cheque so Mike asked to speak to the bank manager who while cashing the cashing the cheque said, "Mike, so you are our member of parliament. When I was a little fellow my ambition was to be a pirate."

"You must be very happy," Mike said. "Few people realize their childhood dreams."

"What do you mean?"

"Well, every time I write a cheque, make a withdrawal or use a self-service machine, there's a fee. I'm waiting for the day when your bank will charge a customer for using its pen to endorse a cheque."

Following that comment Ed headed to Charlie Dunn's Barbershop next door for a haircut. Charlie knew everything there is to know about sports. And even made bets with his customers which team would win the World Series and the Stanley Cup. Seeing that Mike had changed in appearance and although balding in front with long hair in the back and a beard, Charlie said, "Mike, since you became an MP lot of people must not recognize you. Do you mind if I give you a shave and cut off your long hair?"

"If you do, they won't recognize you either," Mike replied and then seeing a bottle on the shelf, which claimed to make hair grow, Mike asked the barber, "That stuff in the bottle, does it really make one's hair grow or is it false advertising?"

"Not only does the stuff make hair grow but it's extraordinary," barber Dunn said. "The last customer, who purchased a bottle, after I gave him the bill, was tearing out his hair for a month."

The following day Mike had some legal work to be done so he said to Belle, "Since I left for Ottawa who is the best lawyer in Edmonton?"

"I still think it's our former mayor Mr. Live when he's sober."

"And the second best?"

"Mr. Live when he's drunk."

"Live? So he has taken to drinking. I'll never use him as my lawyer again."

"Why?

"Because like me, he's getting old and so dumb, that if I ever had to plead insanity, I would use him as Exhibit A."

"Well, if not Live, how about Jack Huff, he's so popular that his clients say if one is in the rough they should see Huff

"Fine, I know him," Mike said and off he went to Huff's office where an appointment wasn't necessary.

Following an introductory conversation, Mike said, "Look, I have a confession to make."

"If you do you are at the wrong place. I do not take confessions, better see Father McCarthy," Huff said.

"Not that kind of a confession," Mike apologized. "Just between the two of us, in absolute confidentiality, I admit that while I was the mayor of Edmonton, I did accept a bribe."

"Specifically what do you do wrong?"

Mike began to sweat, "I accepted $1000 from the contractor who built the water fountain that squirts water in front of City Hall. The contractor also supplied the squirrels which run about in Heritage Park."

"And I assume this contractor contributed financially during your election campaign?"

"He did."

Huff stood up and sat on the edge of his desk and in jest suggested that Ed accept another bribe and that would be his fee.

"Oh, no," Mike said, "I'm getting older and all I want is to have a clear conscience. I want you to witness that I'm sending the $1000 back to the contractor."

Huff notarized the cheque along with a statement, which was attached saying that Mike's conscience bothered him and now, before he died, he could live with peace on his mind.

On Sunday Mike and Belle attended a service at the No Name Universal Church where Reverend Taylor said near the end of his sermon, "Next Sunday I'm going to preach on the subject of *liars*. "With this in mind I would like all of you to read *Chapter 28 of Mark*."

The following Sunday Mike and Belle went to church again and Reverend Taylor put on some pizzas into his sermon when he said, "Now, all of you who have done as I requested and read *Chapter 28 of Mark*, please raise your hands?'

Every hand in the church except Mike's went up so Reverend Taylor said, "You are the people I want to talk too—there is no *28th Chapter of Mark*."

Following the service Belle went home while Ed to visit Rabbi and Mrs. Libowitch who helped Ed during the election campaign, but when Ed arrived, Mrs. Libowitch informed Ed that the rabbi had died recently.

Ed reprimanded Mrs. Libowitch for not notifying him in Ottawa and then said, "Did the rabbi leave a will?"

"Yes."

"And do you recall his last words?"

"You mean before he died?"

"If it's not too painful."

Mrs. Libowitch thought for several seconds and then said, "The rabbi said, 'You can't hit the broadside of a barn with a shotgun'."

Not having a physical examination in over five years Mike next made an appointment to see Dr. Vernon Dark at the Medical Clinic. On the day the appointment arrived a receptionist said, "Sorry, Mr. Bike but Dr. Dark is behind schedule. He'll be with you shortly."

While waiting in the lobby Mike picked up a copy of *The Medical Clinical Dictionary* and was surprised that in the medical community, like in the real estate industry, some words had to be translated in order to be understood by ordinary people. Here is an example.

WORD	MEANING
Artery	Study of painting
Bacteria	Back door to a cafeteria
Barium	What doctor's do when treatment fails
Caesarean Section	A municipality in Rome
Cat Scan	Searching for kitty
Colic	A sheep dog
Coma	A punctuation mark
Congenital	Friendly
D & C	Where Washington is
Diarrhoea	A journal of events
Dilate	To live long
Enema	Not a friend
Genital	Non-Jewish
Varicose	Located nearby
Labour pain	Get hurt at work
Impotent	Distinguished
Prostrate	Flat on your back
Rectum	Damn near killed 'em
Urine	Opposite of you're out
Seizure	Roman Empire
Illegal	A sick bird

When it was Mike's turn to enter Dr. Dark's office he immediately said, "Doctor, since becoming an MP I have developed a problem?"

"What kind of a problem?"

"It's my sex drive."

"Come, come," Dr. Dark said, "Your sex drive is all in your head."

"That's the problem. You'll have to lower it a bit."

As the examination went on Dr. Dark said, "Well, your old ticker is in good shape. Now drop your pants and lean over the table."

"Yes, doctor," Mike said and did what he was told. Mike never called a doctor by his first name as he had no wish to be on a first-name basis with a one who referred to the heart as the *old ticker* and who furthermore stuck his middle finger all the way Mile's rectum.

At the end of the examination Dr. Dark thought Mike should have a wart removed from his neck and went on, "Mike, in addition to the wart you'll have to stop smoking, drinking and having sex or else you'll have a heart attack within a year."

A day passed and Mike went to see Dr, Dark again. "Look, doc," he said. "I'm so miserable to Belle that I might as well be dead. Please, can I smoke just a little?"

"Very well, just a filter a day."

Another day passed and Mike went to see Dr. Dark again. "Look, doc." he said. "I miss my home-made beer, please . . . ."

"All right, just a bottle a day."

Another day passed and Ed approached Dr. Dark for the third time and said, "Listen, doctor I simply must have sex."

"Fine," replied the MD. "And remember, only with Belle—no excitement."

The following afternoon Mike was admitted into the Royal Alec Hospital to remove the wart, which was beginning to look like a cauliflower.

Following the minor surgery Mike was in the recovery room. Seeing a patient next to him he sighed, "Thank God it's over."

"Don't be so sure," the patient in the next bed moaned. "They left a sponge in me and had cut me open a second time."

And the patient on the other side said, "Hey, they had to open me too, to find their instruments."

Just then Dr. Dark who operated on Mike, stuck his head into the room and asked, "Has anyone seen my hat?

No one did.

Meanwhile the tension/stress/strain of being a politician's wife, along with being elderly led Belle to seek psychiatric help. "I'm irritable most of the time and it's difficult for me to get along with people," Belle said to the psychiatrist. Dr. Ben Canoogle, who talked with Belle at length about aging and prescribed a tranquilizer for her nervous condition. Next day Belle returned for the second session with the psychiatrist who asked, "Belle, have you noticed any difference in your condition?"

"Not that I can notice," Belle said. "But I do notice that everybody else, including my husband, has calmed down and they have been much more polite than before."

Dr. Canoogle then said why Belle was feeling the way she did was because aging could be a woman's nightmare unless she had the right attitude. "At your age you have become the invisible woman."

"With that part I agree," Belle replied and gave an example that whenever she was in

In Churchill Square her dog, Dominic, was the focus of attention. "It seems that I'm fading away. My life is changing. There are times when I even speak to my shadow, think Happy Hour is a nap, my memory is shorter and complaining lasts longer, I look for my glasses for an hour only to find that I was wearing them all the time."

"In a society that worships beauty and youth, wrinkles and grey hair can be tickets to obscurity," the psychiatrist said and suggested that to add spice to her life Belle should consider riding a mechanical bull at least once a day."

"I do that already."

"Well, here's something more challenging. I understand you own your own aircraft."

"I do."

"Then why don't you join a skydiving club?"

"I was a member once."

"And what happened?"

"You may not believe this doc. I pulled the parachute cord and nothing happened until I was about 100 feet from the ground and saw a man going up."

"And?"

'So I shouted, 'Hey, there! Do you know anything about parachutes?"

"And?"

"No," the man answered and then he asked me if I knew anything about barbecues."

"Did you get hurt when you landed?"

"Fortunately not because I landed on a trampoline and bounced back into the aircraft."

By the time Mike was released from the hospital it was time for the *Meals on Wheels* Mike Bike *Roast* which took place in the Shaw Convention Centre and it seemed all of Edmonton turned out for the formal dinner that featured roast beef and sumptuous corn delivered from Mr. Fix's farm for the occasion.

The men wore tuxedos, women long dresses as Mike was bagpiped and escorted by two members of the Royal Canadian Mounted Police to the head table.

Reverend Taylor said grace, the 'rubba, tub, tub, thank you for the grub, type and noted that the reason Mike enjoyed sport but never curled was because it says in the *Bible, " Let him who is without sin cast the first stone."*

Belle was the first to roast MIKE and got laughs when she said; "When Mike was asked to seek a political career he said the House of Commons was a place for fools."

Other roasters took their turns and roasting of Mike went on and on and each time the audience burst into laughter. Mike never laughed so hard in his entire life. In the end the master of ceremonies thanked everyone for roasting M P Mike Bike and helping Meals on Wheels. The MC then made short speech about what a wonderful businessman/politician Mike was, what a true and a caring man.

There stood Mike to a thunderous applause, a man from the old school who had goose bumps on top of goose bumps, Edmonton's patriot, an achiever, a breadwinner and hockey promoter with tears of joy running down his cheeks.

It was the only time Belle saw her husband display emotion in public and felt proud while applauding. At the same time she felt sorry for Mike because men, she thought, were not supposed to display emotion. Crying was reserved for women.

Despite a successful roast, *Meals on Wheels* did not meet its objective of raising $20,000. It was $5000 short.

"That does pose a problem", Mike said to the *Meals on Wheels* lady. "I have an idea how we can raise the remaining $5000."

Her curiosity rose, "How?"

"This time let's hold a belly flop contest in the Mill Creek swimming pool and the one with the closest to a perfect dive will receive a sample of your delicious meals for a month as first prize."

"Mike, that's a splendid idea" the *Meals on Wheels* lady said. "When should the contest take place?"

"How about a week from today?"

"Couldn't we make it sooner?"

"Sorry, because I have a mid-week appointment with Pastor Taylor to discuss a personal matter."

During midweek Ed's car pulled up to the No Name Universal Church rectory where once inside Ed said, "Reverend, why is it some people Edmonton are criticizing me since I became a member of parliament? I walk along Jasper Avenue and often, those who supported me at election time avoid me by walking away as if not knowing me?

Even Belle often calls me an old geezer at a time when she knows I have made arrangements to leave her everything I own, including a substantial insurance policy, when I die."

Reverend Taylor who was getting old also, took Mike aside and said, "Mike, let me tell you a story about a pig and a cow. The pig too was complaining to the cow that people always talked about the cow's gentleness and kind eyes while the pigs name came as an insult.

"The pig admitted the cow gave milk, cream, butter and cheese but maintained that a pig gave more. The pig complained that the pigs provided ham, beacon, pork chops, pickled feet and even headcheese out of them.

"The pig could not see why cows were esteemed so much. It was here in the story that the cow replied that maybe it was because cows give while they are still living and pigs are beneficial only after they are dead."

"Good point," Mike said. "That is why I'm so happy that Belle and I are able to contribute to society while we are still living. Hey, Reverend, I'm looking forward to the Belly Flop Contest."

When it was time for the Contest there were 15 local celebrity contestants registered to make waves on a hot summer day. A large crowd gathered at the Mill Creek swimming pool bleachers, each having purchased a $50.00 ticket for the event billed as *Edmonton's Battle of the Bulges*.

Contestants drew numbers as when they would dive. Mike drew #1 and was the first to climb the diving board, flex his muscles and display his physique. A whistle was blown for Mike to make his dive and when did the announcer on the public address system said, "Ladies and gentlemen. I have some good news and some bad news. The good news is that the judges have awarded Mr. Bike's magnificent dive a perfect score."

There was a thunderous applause.

"And the bad news is that he also had a heart attack."

Hearing the PA announcer Pastor Taylor rushed to the spot where Mike landed and along with a lifeguard dragged him out of the pool where he was resuscitated. Seeing Mike in excruciating pain the Reverend leaned over Mike's shoulder and asked, "My friend, have you made peace with God?"

In a faint voice Mike replied, "I didn't know I had an argument with Him."

The Reverend continued, "Mike, do you believe in the Father, Son and Holy Spirit?"

And these were Mike's last words on Planet Earth. "I'm dying and you are asking me riddles."

Minutes later Dr. Dark, who was one of the contestants, pronounced Mike dead with a supplementary announcement, "And that's too bad because Mike was scheduled to receive an honorary doctorate degree from the University of Alberta."

Mike was dead and neighbours were suddenly electrified with the ghastly news. Belle couldn't believe it too as it seemed that just a while ago that Mike's lips were touching hers. In the hours following the death Belle grieved for Mike in her own way as she had never grieved for anyone before.

Belle's parents insisted that Belle spend rest of the summer putting herself together at the Cooking Lake Fishing Hunting and Golfing Resort.

But she declined the invitation as she had to deal with funeral arrangements and other important matters with Pastor Taylor, her lawyer and banker.

Despite the floral tributes, Belle got into an argument with Mike's parents if her husband should be buried or cremated.

They also argued what hymns to sing, the use of an organ or a flute, should the casket be opened or closed, should a private service be held for only the closest or rent the Shaw Convention Centre and accommodate all who may wish to come for what ever reason people come to a funeral. In the end it was agreed to hold a public funeral at the No Name Universal Church and that the wooden coffin would be open.

Among the hymns to be sung were *Amazing Grace* and *How Great Thou Art* accompanied with the organ. After the burial there would be a wake in the Norwood Community Hall and lunch served.

The obituary notice in the newspapers *in* part read: "Rather than flowers, Mrs. Bike suggests donations be made to *Meals on Wheels*."

Edmonton bid farewell to Mike Bike in a simple service remembering him as a realtor/politician whose stage was the city of Edmonton and Canada.

Some arrived early to pay their respect. Sammy Helper, who knew Mike all his life, flew in from Calgary and publicly said, "I have lost a true friend."

Outside the church several passers-by's enquiring about the service reacted with indifference and even contempt.

Although the mortality rate for realtors and politicians is 100% a discontented constituent said, "Couldn't happen to a nicer crook."

"He's dead? Who cares? Let them make a potpourri from his fingernails and hair," said another.

It is true that when Mike was alive there were people who said nasty things about him but as soon as he died, they praised him. This occurred when the former mayor Live said, "Mike Bike was the kindest and most generous man I have ever known. Neither Heaven or, oh, yes, hockey, will not be the same with Mike there."

Shortly after 1:00 p. m. church bells rang and a motorcade delivered Belle and Mike's's parents. They made their way in silence up a flight of stairs into the church and then the front pews where Mike's body lay in front of them in an open casket.

Mourners listened to tributes as the mood of the service swung back and forth between laughter and grief. They all had to pause to shed tears or regain their composure as Pastor Taylor urged everyone to celebrate the, "Man who put Edmonton on the map of Canada and *Meals on Wheels* out of debt."

"Belle, Ed loved you very much," Pastor Taylor said, his voice slightly slurred from a stroke. "We all know that, so don't cry much. Think of Mike up there in Heaven with St. Peter and Rabbi Libowitch."

Pastor Taylor then read words from the *Bible* and there wasn't a dry eye in the church as he said, "Mike Bike, this isn't the final chapter of your life. May your soul enter Heaven and may you rest in peace."

Then as the bagpipes played loudly and the drums beat slowly six realtors picked up the coffin covered with white linen and marched to Hainstock's Funeral Home and Crematorium where Mike's ashes turned to dust. In a flash Mike went straight to the Pearly Gates where Saint Peter, the gate keeper, was waiting to interview him.

But Mike had little peace in Heaven initially because when he arrived at the Pearly Gates there was a line-up and Mike hated line-ups even on Planet Earth.

St. Peter interviewed the first, second and third and then eventually asked another, "Where are you from?"

"America," The elderly man in the lineup answered.

"And what have you done to deserve admission to Heaven?"

"I have been a bus driver for many years."

"You've had too many accidents and have to go to Hell," St. Peter said, as the Pearly Gates remained closed.

St. Peter then turned to the man in front of Ed and said, "And where are you from?'

"Germany."

"And what have you done to deserve admission here?"

"I've been a lawyer all my life, sir, and have taken part in many complex lawsuits."

St. Peter started to escort the lawyer inside when the lawyer began to protest that his untimely death had to be some sort of mistake. "I'm much too young to die. I'm only thirty-five," he said.

St. Peter agreed that 35 did seem a bit young to be entering the Pearly Gates, and then checked the lawyer's profile. When St. Peter returned, he said to the attorney, "I'm afraid the mistake must be yours, my son. We have verified your age on the basis of the number of hours you've billed your clients and you're at least 88. You must go to Hell too."

Mike didn't wait for the question when it was his turn to be interviewed so he turned to St. Peter, knelt before him and said, "Look. I'm from Edmonton, Canada. Do I have to go to Hell too?"

St. Peter took of his glasses, shook his head and the said, "Living in Edmonton you have already been there," and along with a devout priest from Argentina was told to go inside the Pearly Gates.

"Father, here are the keys to one of the nicest suites;" St. Peter said to the priest and to Ed, "And you Mr. Summer, here are the keys to Heaven's penthouse where angels drift about, play harps and sing. It's a very nice place."

This upset Father Garcia and to St, Peter said, "I don't understand this. I have dedicated my entire life preaching the word of God and . . ."

"Listen, Father," St. Peter interrupted. "Priests are a dime a dozen here but this is the first politician we have seen in a long, long time."

The following Sunday parishioners at the No Name Universal Church prayed to St. Peter, the gatekeeper, to have just a glimpse of Mike Bike in Heaven. Their wish was granted but to their horror the following Sunday they saw on a huge screen Ed with a beautiful blond on his lap.

"Ed! Ed!" they cried out. "How come you behave this way in Heaven, when you never chased women in Edmonton?"

Ed replied, "Listen, you people below, the blond is not my reward. I'm her punishment."

CHAPTER 10

Belle missed Mike terribly and shortly after the funeral developed PMS—post mortem syndrome. During the grieving period Belle did not adapt to the changing times. She found it difficult to finance real estate properties as banks one after another called their loans on buildings Belle owned or inherited. Belle had no intention of marrying again and quit writing columns for the *Journal*.

Six months after bank loans were called Belle was no longer a proud owner of Bike rental properties which stretched across Canada and Western United States. The Skydome and CN Tower in Toronto, the private jet, Toronto Maple Leafs were also taken away from her. An economist called Belle's loss, "Collapse of an Empire."

As soon as bankruptcy papers were signed Belle accepted an offer from her father-in-law to manage the Cooking Lake Fishing, Hunting and Golfing Resort. The senior Bike's decided to take a year off for a vacation in Europe and at the same time trace their Polish genealogical roots.

The Fishing Hunting Golfing Resort complex consisted of a main lodge with a lobby, an office, restaurant and sleeping quarters for thirty guests. On each side of the lodge were twenty rustic cabins, which faced and had an easy access to Cooking Lake. For decoration all cabins had bearskin at the entrance and exciting wildlife pictures, and wooden chairs that when you leaned back left an impression, even through a jacket.

The entire complex had signs posted. Near cabin # 01, the sign read: *DON'T CLEAN FISH ON PICNIC TABLES.* Near cabin #02: *IF YOU SEE BAMBI, PLEASE DON'T HIT HER WITH YOUR VEHICLE.* Near #03: *MAKE CERTAIN YOU HAVE A FISHING OR HUNTING LICENSE.* Near #04: *NEAR THIS SPOT A TITANIC WHITE FISH WAS CAUGHT AND RELEASED.* Near #05: *THE PRINCE OF WALES SELPT IN THIS CABIN.* Near #06: *GEORGE BERNARD SHAW WAS GOING TO SLEEP HERE BUT WE HAD NO VACANCY.*

A week into her management Belle booked a group of Americans who were going to stay at the lodge for a week. When they arrived Belle thought the occasion called for a roaring fire in the lobby fireplace. Unfortunately Belle forgot the damper. The wood in the fireplace was very dry and the lobby soon filled with suffocating smoke.

Belle took an elaborate windup and caught the leader of the American group head-on with a bucket of water as he was descending a staircase. A volunteer helped Belle but he pitched the bucket to high and drenched the polar bear skin above the fireplace mantel.

The following day Belle sent the bear skin to Edmonton where a furrier undertook to restore the damaged treasure. Belle attached a note to the bear skin which read: "Please Be Careful. It's Priceless." Belle also enclosed a 15-year snapshot of the original skin on the wall above the fireplace.

The bearskin returned within a week and Belle was surprised that the furrier could do little to the treasure.

A note attached to the fur read: "Your priceless fur is now worth $12.00. Secondly, we regret to inform you that for the past 15 years it was hung upside down."

The bearskin returned on the same day that Belle had an unusual experience as a resort manager. This occurred when she found an empty suitcase with a baby cougar next to it. The cub appeared dead so Belle stuffed the animal into the suitcase and was going to bury it as soon as it got dark outside. But within that space of time a guest asked Belle if she had found a green coloured suitcase.

"I certainly did," Belle said. "Here it is."

When the guest opened the suitcase the cub jumped out and ran through the lodge hallway. What had happened was that when the cub was placed into the suitcase it was stunned, not dead. At any rate several of the guests panicked. One even said, "Hand me a gun! I'll shoot the animal!"

While guests were searching for a gun Belle decided to give the animal a chase with a broom. She tried to guide the cub through an exit door but the animal decided to head for the kitchen where it caused havoc with groceries and utensils on the shelves. Finally the cub made an exit by jumping out a kitchen window that was open.

Belle could chase a cub cougar but one thing she lacked was report with the resort cooks. For instance, Alice Logan was a cook at the resort for ten years. Mrs. Logan was an excellent cook and made best ice cubes one ever tasted. Her specialty was fried water but one day she got fancy with her cooking and screwed-up the cornflakes.

To Mrs. Logan a balanced meal was one which the guests had a 50-50 chance of surviving. She sliced tomatoes by throwing them through a screen door. One day she had turkey on the menu and those who ordered a meal were tickled. Mrs. Logan had forgotten to take off the feathers. Things between Belle and Mrs. Logan came to a head, however, when the health inspector arrived and discovered a crate containing 24 dozen eggs which were left near the kitchen stove and chicks began hatching. Seeing the chicks' pop up one after another Mrs Logan said to Belle, "Why don't you say something interesting to the chickens?"

Mrs. Logan got on top of the crate and was about to say "Chickens of the World Unite for better laying egg laying condition." But instead fired Mrs. Logan for incompetence.

When the new cook arrived at the lodge she didn't last long. Big "Alice" Rock fell over one of her meatballs and injured her spleen. Belle called 911 and an ambulance took Alice to the hospital.

When Big "Alice" Rock felt better was transferred home where she lay in the sun on a Cooking Lake beach. Alice laid in the sun often, the heat that summer was so intense that she became petrified and spent the rest of her life in isolation.

Why was this cook, in the prime of her life, so afflicted? Because, according to geologists, she was deposited on Planet Earth during the Ice Age.

Belle didn't believe this theory however, but one suggested by Chief Wondering Spirit of the nearby Cree Indian Band who said that why Big "Alice" Rock was so afflicted this way was because she had stolen a blanket while employed at the Sandman Hotel where she previously worked in the housekeeping department.

Today Alice "Big" Rock is an imposing sight and site and sticks out like thumb for the entire world to see, like the ruins of some feudal castle crumbling with decay. Now tourists to Edmonton can see Alice "Big" Rock as an icon where highways 2 and 16 converge

The next cook Belle hired was Tapioca Wilson. Ms Wilson was called Tapioca not because she could be made in a minute but because she enjoyed everything that was sweet. One day Belle saw that Tapioca was depressed so she asked, "What is the matter? Your cooking is excellent."

"I can't believe this." Tapioca said. "Some of the employees are spreading lies that before I joined the staff at the Cooking Lake Fishing Hunting and Golfing Resort, I had twins."

"Relax," Belle said. "I make it a rule to believe only one-half of what I hear."

Actually Tapioca was a wonderful cook so Belle said to her, "Your pies are delicious."

"Thank you."

"And the half-moon decoration on the crust, how did you make them?"

Belle was surprised when Tapioca answered, "By using my false teeth."

Tapioca was soon known throughout Alberta as an exceptional cook. For example she wrapped spaghetti around meatballs and called them, "Hot yo yo's."

She could cook up an order of whitefish in 10 minutes, whitefish steak, whitefish croquettes and a whitefish salad. Once a year those who ate her fishmeals got the urge to go to the Saskatchewan River and spawn.

One day Belle found Tapioca holding a rope in her hand so she said, "Tapioca, what are you doing?"

"That's my weather gauge to cook meals by." Tapioca said.

"How on earth can you possibly forecast the weather with a rope?"

"Simple," Tapioca said. "When the rope swings back and forth, it's windy so I cook spaghetti. When the rope gets wet, it's raining, so I cook pork chops."

Tapioca Wilson became a permanent cook at the resort and that was great. It gave Belle more free time to socialize with her guests.

One of the groups Belle did public relations with consisted of three members of a hunting club from Los Angeles. Since the Californians were not use to the northern Canadian climate, and handling guns, the casualty list was rather formidable.

One hunter had his hand in a sling; another was hopping on his foot, the third looked like a bear mauled him.

"Cheer up," Belle said to the three hunters. Then turning to the one with a bag, went on, "Judging by the buldge in your bag, you're not coming back empty handed."

The hunter carrying the bag said, "That's our hunting dog."

The following day the tree hunters convinced Belle to go hunting with them while they tracked down a bear. "All right, I'll go," Belle conceded reluctantly and went on, "But if you start wrestling with a bear and look around, and don't see nobody, that's me."

On their last day at the resort the three hunters were resting by the lobby fireplace in their pyjamas when one announced to the other two and Belle, "I'm restless. I'll go for a walk before I go to sleep."

The other two hunters didn't fret of his non-appearance for an hour when one glanced at his watch and said, "Mmmm, I wonder what's eating Ernie?"

What happened was that Ernie had met a bear, got frightened and ran back to the lodge as fast as he could with the bear behind him. Just as he reached the lodge Ernie slipped and fell. The bear was going so fast that it skidded right through the front door and into the lodge. Ernie got up and closed the door from inside and then shouted to his friends and Belle, "Skin this one while I go and get another!"

With that Ernie picked up a bottle of rum and a gun from his room. Five minutes later Ernie took three shots but before he put the bottle down the second bear began chasing him.

Fortunately for Ernie he could run faster than the bear and when he returned to the lodge said, "You know something? You won't believe this, but I ran away from a bear in my pyjamas."

"Stop! Stop!" Belle said. "How did the bear get into your pyjamas?"

"Ah jeez," replied Ernie and went straight to his room.

As for the first bear and it wasn't easy, Belle had other guests in the lodge coax the animal to make an exit through a rear door.

Next, a wife accompanied a prominent physician from Calgary when they stayed at the lodge and on the first day the couple went hunting alone but returned empty-handed.

"I didn't kill a thing today," the husband said.

On the second day the doctor's wife was all togged in fancy hunting clothing, with a smoking rifle in her hands, and a look of unholy glee on her face. "I must have hit something." she said to her husband. "Just listen to the language Belle is using."

On the third day the doctor and his wife were dressed in buckskin jackets and each wore a necklace made of moose and bear teeth.

When they came to a ravine the doctor sounded his moose-call but no moose burst into a clearing. Instead a pack of mice scurried into view.

"Damnation," muttered the doctor to his wife. "I told you to buy me a moose—call and not a mouse-call."

The doctor was greatly disappointed because he had been a force to reckon with in the highly competitive world of moose calling. "One has to sound like a cow moose in heat. It's a call for love," he said.

Hunters use horns ranging from tolled birch bark to fancy miniature alpine horn-like things to mellow out the tone. Cupped hands are for amateurs. Some hunters even pinch their nostrils with two fingers to get a nasal sound.

It was the following day that two farmers from Regina were vacationing at the resort and after renting a boat, tolled in the open water but the motor went dead. Before they could say, "It takes two bushels of oats to buy a cup of coffee" fog set in on Cooking Lake and they could not see land. Most farmers in Saskatchewan are sharp, however, and had the motor running again.

At the same time another boat came by, they hailed it, and one of the Saskatchewan fishermen asked, "Hey, there! Can you tell us which way to Edmonton from here?"

The operator of the second boat, which was equipped with expensive electronic equipment, shouted back, "Just a minute and I'll get an exact reading!"

One of the Saskatchewan fishermen scoffed, "Don't bother getting technical just point with your finger."

When the Saskatchewan vacationers returned to the lodge Belle pontificated them for taking a vacation at a time when they could be doing farm work. "You've got large spread of land near Regina. You could make a lot of money if you would spend more time cultivating it. And, hey! Haven't you heard about the starving in the Third World?"

One of the farmers took out a map of the world from his jacket pocket and after examining it said, "Mrs. Winter-Bike, you'll notice on this map that two-thirds of the earth is water and one-third is land. So it seems to me that man is supposed to fish two-thirds of the time and farm one-third."

What could Belle do with that reasoning?

Nothing.

Overall Belle Winter-Bike like her husband Mike had a happy life despite the up's and down's. And Belle's life, like Mike's, had a sad ending. It seems that one evening a laxative salesman from Vancouver named Bill Brennan stopped at the resort to relax and do some golfing. Mr. Brennan didn't go golfing that evening because he was tired so he went straight to bed forgetting his briefcase in the lobby.

Belle became curious and opened the briefcase to see what was inside and found packages marked (Made in China 1995) of chocolate-coated candy and took several packs thinking the salesman wouldn't miss them.

Shortly after sunrise the Mr Brennan was about to go golfing when he noticed Belle sitting on a chair in the lobby.

"Good morning," Brennan said but Belle kept on looking straight ahead ignoring the guest. Perturbed the salesman got in touch with a security guard and asked, "What have I done to Mrs. Winter—Bike that she refuses to speak to me?"

"Sir." the security guard replied, "Belle Winter-Bike died overnight. We're just waiting for her to shut off so we can bury her."

Following the funeral Belle was met at the Pearly Gate by St. Peter, the gate keeper, and asked Belle why she deserved to go to Heaven at a time when she lost all her earthly assets.

Belle replied, "Not all, I have a probated letter which is witnessed by my pastor, banker and lawyer. Do you want to read what's in it?"

And when the letter was opened St. Peter put on his reading glasses and read it which in part read:

"I, Belle Winter-Bike had my will probated and although I have lost I my earthly assets I'm still entitled to the insurance policy that my husband left me with a rider that says, 'In the even my wife's death the proceeds of the insurance policy are to go towards eliminating poverty throughout the world.'

Minutes later Belle joined her husband Mike in Heaven.